ALSO BY CHO NAM-JOO

Kim Jiyoung, Born 1982

CHO NAM-JOO

SAHA

TRANSLATED BY JAMIE CHANG

SCRIBNER

LONDON NEW YORK SYDNEY TORONTO NEW DELHI

First published in the United States by Liveright publishing corporation,
a division of W. W. Norton & Company, 2023

First published in Great Britain by Scribner,
an imprint of Simon & Schuster UK Ltd, 2022
This edition published 2023

Copyright © 사하맨션 (SAHA MANSION) by 조남주 (Cho Nam-joo), 2019

English Language Copyright © Jamie Chang

Originally published in Korea by Minumsa Publishing Co., Ltd., Seoul.

Agreement with Cho Nam-joo c/o Minumsa Publishing Co., Ltd.
in association with The Grayhawk Agency Ltd.

The right of Cho Nam-joo to be identified as the author
of this work has been asserted in accordance with the
Copyright, Designs and Patents Act, 1988.

SCRIBNER and design are registered trademarks of The Gale Group, Inc.,
used under licence by Simon & Schuster Inc.

1 3 5 7 9 10 8 6 4 2

Simon & Schuster UK Ltd
1st Floor
222 Gray's Inn Road
London WC1X 8HB

www.simonandschuster.co.uk
www.simonandschuster.com.au
www.simonandschuster.co.in

Simon & Schuster Australia, Sydney
Simon & Schuster India, New Delhi

This book is a work of fiction.
Names, characters, places and incidents are either a
product of the author's imagination or are used fictitiously.
Any resemblance to actual people living or dead,
events or locales is entirely coincidental.

A CIP catalogue record for this book is available from the British Library

Paperback ISBN: 978-1-3985-1002-9
eBook ISBN: 978-1-3985-1001-2
eAudio ISBN: 978-1-3985-1380-8

Book design by Beth Steidle

Printed and Bound in the UK using 100% Renewable
Electricity at CPI Group (UK) Ltd

WALL

1 ◄──── UNITS ──────── A

PARKING

ENTRANCE-
SIGN

CUSTODIAN'S
OFFICE

COMMUNAL
WATER TAP

GARBAGE DUMP

VEGETABLE GARDEN

MACHINE
ROOM

UNITS

PLAYGROUND

14

21 ◄──────────── B ──────────► 15

SAHA ESTATES

THE SIBLINGS

DO-KYUNG BLACKED OUT, THEN WOKE WITH A START,
blacked out. He woke up when Su's hand carefully slipped out
of his, and at the quiet tread of a small animal passing by. But
then sleep pulled him under again, and he dreamed an endless
stream of scenes, pouring like grains of sand through an hour-
glass. Was he dreaming or was he awake, or dead? He couldn't
tell. He alternately fought to let go, and to hang on.

The night grew ever deeper. At one point, when it was so
deep it seemed fathomless, something forced its way up Do-
kyung's esophagus. Bitter swill shot to his tongue and dripped
from his nostrils. Do-kyung capped a hand over his mouth,
groped around for the door handle with the other. The car
door swung open as vomit burst out of him. The bilious liquid
poured forth without end, not stopping even after he'd soaked
the ground below him. He pounded on his chest and managed
to cease the retching, but then a burning as violent as fire shot
up from the pit of his stomach to his throat.

Foul, sticky fluids dripping from his mouth, nose, and eyes, Do-kyung wrapped his hands around his neck and turned to look at Su in the passenger seat. She was lying very straight on her back. Skin so white it bore a tinge of blue, hands gathered primly, awkward smile. She looked like a wax doll. Do-kyung carefully placed a hand on her chest. Her heart wasn't beating. He held a finger below her nose, but felt nothing.

The long, low headlights of a faraway car emitted a white, undulating wave of light that turned orange, then white again. Spreading dim and wide, the lights enlarged and lengthened the limbs of a tree. Shadows like the antlers of an old and solitary animal grew smaller and darker as if a soul were moving through them. Do-kyung stared blankly at the outlines of the shadows as they grew vivid, then came the terrifying realization: *The shadow is getting darker. The light is getting closer. Someone's coming.*

A dirt road leading to a deserted park. A lone luxury sedan parked askew. Inside, a woman who could be asleep or dead. A sight to raise suspicion in anyone. Do-kyung's mind knew as instantly as a sheet of paper catches fire that he had to run, but his body could not leave the car. He reached for Su's hand but yanked it back before they touched. He couldn't take her or leave her. So Do-kyung locked the doors from the inside, got out of the car, and tested the door to make sure it was locked. Su was now a being completely different from Do-kyung. She lay perfectly still beyond everyone's reach, like an illusion, like a doll in a glass coffin.

Above, on the hill next to the roadside, was a mess of rocks, branches, exposed roots jutting out every which way, and below, on the shoulder of the road, was loose dirt that people got stuck in and skidded off even when it wasn't raining. Do-kyung chose the latter. His feet picked up speed in no time.

A STREETLIGHT OVERHEAD crackled and blinked. Do-kyung had run as fast as his legs would take him, wherever his feet could find footing, and it wasn't until a car zipped by with a sustained beep that he realized he was standing in the middle of a four-lane road. He whipped his head around and looked as far as his eyes could see, then hurried to the other side. When he reached the sidewalk his legs gave out.

His right knee scraped the coarse sidewalk, tearing his light cotton pants and breaking skin. Bright red blood seeped into his cream-colored pants. Do-kyung gathered his palms over his knee and pressed his brow against the back of his hands. In the brief time he was curled up on the ground, the tattered fabric of his pants glued to the scrape. Carefully, he tried to peel off the loose threads by rubbing with the tip of his finger. Clotted scabs came off, springing fresh drops of vivid red. A groan slipped through his clenched jaw.

Su came to mind only then. Her hot, dry lips on the nape of his neck. Running his hands over the goose bumps on the back of his neck, he looked up at the park across the street. *She's still there.* Su and Do-kyung used to drive up the dirt road, and hike the rest of the way to the top where the park was. It was a steep, narrow trail that led to not much—a clearing with a few benches, no view, nothing to do, and no one around. Su and Do-kyung had liked the park all the more for it and visited often. Do-kyung left Su there and ran.

IT WAS A supermarket cleaning job. Jin-kyung had wondered why the job was on a Saturday, when supermarkets were the busiest; when she got there, she realized it had gone out of business. The place had closed suddenly due to contract renewal troubles. The refrigerators and freezers were shut down with the contents still inside, and it was clear cleaning had never been a priority to begin with. Vegetables and fruits had liquefied, and some of the milk cartons had exploded under pressure of decomposition. No words could describe the stench of rotting meat. Mold, vermin of every imaginable variety, pools of festering juices on the floor. One of the cleaners retched the moment they walked in.

CLEANING WENT ON well into the night. Jin-kyung stayed behind to finish up, and the team leader handed her a large plastic bag and said, "Overtime pay." She filled it with beverages in plastic bottles she'd set aside when cleaning out the back.

"They're clean. They don't expire for a while, and the cap seals weren't broken," the team leader said. "I'm going to take some myself," she insisted as she loaded her bag. "I wouldn't have been able to do this sort of thing at your age. There's no shame in this, you know. This is all money. Make a lot of money. Work like your life depends on it. That way you'll at least get to be L2. In the meantime, drink this."

"But there's no one to drink all the . . ."

Jin-kyung thought of the people she could no longer describe as "not around anymore" because they were just plain "gone." She hadn't seen Do-kyung in two days.

THERE WERE TWO classes of people in Town: L and L2. The ones with Town citizenship were referred to as Ls, or Citizens.

These were people above a certain level of financial status who had knowledge or skills that Town required. Underage residents were recognized as Citizens only if they had parents or legal sponsors who were Citizens.

L2 visas were issued to those without citizenship qualifications who had a clean criminal record. Applicants went through a brief interview and physical examination. They were referred to around Town as L2, and their visas were good for two years. Two years were all they got. They were welcome to look for work in all areas during those two years without fear of deportation, but most workplaces that sought L2 labor were construction sites, warehouses, cleaning companies, and other hard labor for little pay. When the two years were up, L2s had to go through another round of interviews and physical exams to extend their visas.

Most L2s were natives who put themselves through the degradation because they didn't have the qualifications to make Citizen and simply couldn't leave their hometowns. When the L2s had children they couldn't afford to raise, those children became L2s as well.

Jin-kyung wasn't even an L2, but a Saha—she wasn't anyone or anything deserving of a category. Saha was what they were called even if they didn't live in Saha Estates, which Jin-kyung assumed the name came from. The term seemed to say, *This is as far as you get.*

WALKING THROUGH THE main gate of the Saha Estates, Jin-kyung scanned Block A, starting wide and slowly narrowing her scope: the seventh-floor walkway, Do-kyung's apartment, his front door, and the kitchen window. All the windows of his apartment were pitch-black, as if he'd closed up the place and left on purpose. The exhaustion of a day's labor, the ache in her arms and legs, and the weight of the plastic bags in both hands hit her all at once. Stretched thin by the weight of the beverages, the handles were digging into her fingers.

The bag in her right hand ripped, sending the plastic bottles rolling down into the front yard. Jin-kyung bent down to grab them, arms extending every which way and losing grip on the other plastic bag. Trying to catch the bottles from the second bag, she dropped the ones she'd already picked up. Jin-kyung let her hands dangle by her sides and watched the contents scatter away. The night breeze picked up the ripped plastic bag and held it in the air.

"Lost your marbles, and for this?" The custodian's office door opened slowly with a squeak. The old man picked up the plastic bag that hadn't ripped, and ambled around the yard picking up the bottles. When the bag was full, he filled his own pockets, tucked two under his armpits, and held two in his hands. He headed back to his office.

"There's another one by the faucets," he said without looking back.

Jin-kyung picked up the runaway bottle resting by the water pail near one of the faucets, and followed the old man. He put the juice in his refrigerator. There wasn't much space, since it was stocked with food containers, bottled water, and bottled soju. He moved the containers around to make room, but could only fit two bottles in the end. He opened the freezer and stared into it for a while.

"Want one?" he asked, closing the freezer door.

Jin-kyung shook her head, but the old man twisted the

cap open for her anyway. On the small television on his desk, ads for an apartment complex, dish soap, a dietary supplement, and a movie trailer came on, followed by the wrap-up news. Jin-kyung sat on the edge of the desk and took a sip of the juice. It was warm and sour. She couldn't tell if it had gone bad, or if that was what it was supposed to taste like. The old man rolled back and forth in his chair and took big, noisy gulps of the juice and then sighed contentedly as if it were strong liquor.

The old man didn't drink from the communal faucets in the yard. His fridge was always stocked full of expensive bottled water, which he used to cook with as well. In the summer, he would watch disdainfully as Jin-kyung drank straight from a faucet with her head craned sideways. One time, he came over and turned off the tap while she was drinking and said something cryptic: "Ever wonder why people at Saha die so easily? Why all the birth defects? You think it's just because they can't go to the hospital?"

On the TV, a female anchor relayed the accidents and crimes of the day, her lips smiling subtly.

"A woman was found dead in a car by a park entrance. Police are investigating. Ten p.m. last night, a Citizen out for a walk in the Compound Third Street Park near Saha Estates found the body and called the police. The body has been identified as a pediatrician in her early thirties who was reported missing by her family. She'd been missing for two days when she was found. The police reported in a press briefing that the car belonged to the deceased, and signs of sexual assault found on the body suggest rape and murder."

Jin-kyung slammed her bottle on the old man's desk, juice

spilling over on impact. Su. Su was dead. Su was dead and Do-kyung had been gone for days. *I must find Do-kyung*, Jin-kyung thought, but didn't know how to go about finding a man who didn't own a cell phone, had no friends, and hadn't been doing much lately besides drawing in his sketch pad. She got up to go search the park first.

"Where are you going?" the old man asked.

Jin-kyung paused for a moment and then started for the gates.

"Hold it!" the old man shouted urgently. It was the first time she had heard him raise his voice to this level. Always aloof and indifferent, the custodian lived in Saha Estates, his pay came from the Saha Estates residents, and yet he seemed to look down on them all. *I'm not like you*, his attitude suggested, *I have nothing to do with you, I don't care*. And yet here he was, taking great strides toward Jin-kyung, grabbing her by the arm.

"Don't go."

Jin-kyung looked him straight in the eye. His eyes were a light, almost faded brown. His pupils weren't dilated despite the darkness that surrounded them. Questions flooded her mind as she looked into his pupils that reminded her of wrinkles and age rings, but she didn't ask.

"I don't know what's going on, Jin-kyung," he said, breaking the silence as if to respond to her unarticulated questions. "Nothing good comes of groundless panic."

There was something solid in the old man's grip. Jin-kyung had heard he'd crossed the border into Town over a decade ago. The trajectory that led him to Saha was likely as punishing as Jin-kyung's. Did he have family? His old eyes saw something young eyes could not.

The old man's large hand loosened its grip on Jin-kyung's arm.

"Thanks for the juice," he said.

THE SAHA ESTATES

The village had lived off the fish farms for generations. One year, red tide began to devastate the fish farms, forcing them to close down one by one. Without decent tourist attractions to bring in money or a port for trading of substantial scale, villagers began leaving their hometown in search of a livelihood. Then one corporation made a deal with the local government. Office buildings and factories sprang up, followed by apartment complexes and an infusion of young people. Children played in new playgrounds, and yellow school buses meandered through the narrow, winding roads that now ran through the residential areas. The corporation pushed aggressively for expansion in the IT and biotech fields, and this yielded swift results. The village—now a bustling Town/city—received international attention. People started referring to it by the name of the corporation.

But the growth of Town did not mean opportunities for local businesses. The subsidiaries kept designing and erecting more buildings, and after surviving the competition they took over distribution lines and banks, keeping the money within the conglomerate. The tax benefits and support agreements that the desperate local government hastily agreed to came back to poison the local economy. Eventually the local government filed for bankruptcy. And after an interminable fight in the courts, the village was sold to the corporation. Bought out. This marked the birth of an odd city-state that was not quite company or country.

The life of one city had ended and a new chapter had begun, but there weren't any palpable changes. The city had been functioning like a corporation for over a decade before it declared independence. Most residents who were employees of the corporation and its subsidiaries went to work at the same offices, sent their children to the same schools, and maintained the same lives they had before. But the non-employees were gripped with a fear they couldn't name. Many quickly moved to the mainland. Protests small and large were held, demanding protective measures against foreseeable calamities, but the corporation insisted they would cross those bridges when they got to them.

The head of the corporation, a man approaching eighty, gave a city-wide address. "I'm only a businessman. All I know is how to make money," he said. "I bought the city to foster an environment without regulations. Where people can earn what they deserve. I gave my youth to this company and city, but I don't intend to turn it into my own kingdom. Town belongs to you."

It was this address that gave the little city-nation the nickname "Town."

Just before the official takeover, the corporation had issued a great volume of stocks under the guise of securing funds. Those who saw value and potential in the corporation that was about to become its own country formed investment firms and bought the stocks and gathered investors. Most of the investment came from native Town residents. The corporation became a government branch called the Ministry of Means and Industry when Town became a nation. The corporation vanished, which turned its stock into garbage. The airport, railways, roads, and public housing were sold to foreign investors for cheap. The majority of the foreign investors were relations of the company executives.

Town opted for a government of co-ministers. Specialists in education, law, labor, corporation, defense, culture, and environment sent in multiple names for recommendation, which were then discussed behind closed doors among incumbent ministers and candidates to put together a seven-minister council, one per field. The identities of the ministers were kept strictly confidential, and supposedly even the head of the former corporation, "founder" of Town, didn't know who they were. The head of the corporation only appointed one person as spokesperson for the Council of Ministers.

The highest level of income, a near-tenure position, absolute power. But status that couldn't be flaunted was no status at all, and a life led under the disguise of a fake job and identity had to be stressful. Leaking confidential information about the Council or revealing someone's status as minister meant a maximum sentence. One of the founding ministers revealed classified information about the Council and himself in a private gathering and was executed in public. They made an example of him, was the prevailing opinion.

To quell the reasonable fear and confusion among the public, the Council of Ministers proposed a provisional bill simply referred to as "Special Law" and passed it. Television and radio channels were consolidated, as was the press. Certain departments were eliminated at the university. Professors, researchers, and students of certain fields suddenly found themselves without means. Location, type of establishment, and the personal history of the owners were all grounds for shutting down shops and firms, and there was no way to contest the Council's decisions.

When more than three adults gathered on weekends or holidays, they needed to receive clearance first. This applied to religious organizations as well. Some words were prohibited from printing or saying out loud. Context was immaterial; mere expression was grounds enough for punishment. There were songs that couldn't be sung out loud, books that couldn't be read, roads that couldn't be taken. People not to meet. Strange policies so commonly enforced called common sense into question.

The native residents were all promised citizenship when the city was first bought out. The promise was not kept. The Council of Ministers decided upon a citizenship and visa system to guard against illegal entry. Those who led quiet lives on the land where they had always lived were ordered to vacate, and what little they had was seized as public property. The "Special Law" did not check this process in any way. The policy targeted native residents, turning them into loitering criminals swarming Town. Town holding cells soon ran out of space. Proceedings were expedited, and summary indictments sentenced native residents to deportation in great numbers. The measure was intended to bring immediate order to the Town, the Council announced, but the harsh policies remained after order was achieved.

The Council of Ministers continued to operate the same way. When disease, accident, or death created a vacancy in the Council, a new minister was appointed to one of the seven seats, of which nothing was made public. The only affiliated person to appear in public was the original spokesperson that the head of the corporation had appointed in the beginning, who was terribly young when he took the post and was able to capably fulfill his duties to the present.

THE RESIDENTIAL AREAS formerly occupied by the deportees were swiftly leveled in the name of redevelopment, but the Saha Estates redevelopment kept getting postponed. In the meantime, a handful of people who couldn't be Citizens but didn't want to leave began hiding out in Saha Estates. The demolition notice that hung at the gate was periodically updated, each time with a later schedule. At some point, the Saha Estates residents removed the notice. A new notice was hung and removed, another hung, removed. A notice warning not to remove the notice was hung and also removed. After a few unseen tugs-of-war, the unthinkable happened: no more notices.

Not long after the notices stopped, the plumbing and gas lines for each unit were cut off. But the faucets in the yard overflowed with just a turn of the tap. Sewage drained well. Thanks to the solar panels on the roof, the electricity wasn't completely cut off, either. There was the occasional power outage in the buildings, but no one complained. No police or government employees came poking around. Saha residents were able to work at nearby construction sites, warehouses, and other similarly filthy, dangerous workplaces. Life was livable. Those who came to the Saha Estates for temporary shelter began nesting with small furnishings and appliances. Stoves were adjusted to connect to LPG tanks. On the doors, hook-and-eye latches were installed on the inside and padlocks were hung on the outside. More windows began to light up at night.

As in any other apartment complex, the residents of Saha Estates silently acknowledged each other, patted the heads of children they didn't know, asked which unit they lived in, if their electricity situation was okay, and whether gas was leaking from their tanks. Rumors circulated: this side got the most sun, that floor was deserted and spooky, so-and-so's family moved units three times. Then an official residents' association formed at someone's suggestion. A steering committee was put together and a representative elected. Each unit paid a fee to hire a custodian to manage the facilities. That was forty years ago.

Town.

The country that did not accept citizens without capital, skills, or expertise. The country with the most comprehensive semiconductor core technology, handheld devices, and displays, the greatest number of patents in the field of vaccines, pharmaceuticals, and medical devices, and the largest, most advanced biotech research center staffed with the brightest team. The only country to adopt a Council of seven co-ministers for its government. The country entirely run by seven ministers lording over the puppet Parliament, who never revealed their identities, much less engaged with the public. The country that did not belong to any international organization or regional union. The smallest, strangest country, which went by the name of Town. In this rigid land that outsiders could not access and no one wanted to leave, in this mysterious, reclusive state, the Saha Estates was the only secret passageway.

HANGING OFF THE iron railing on the ground floor of Block A was a pair of rubber gloves. They belonged to Granny Konnim. She hung rubber gloves, kerchiefs, and rags on the railing from time to time. The old custodian and the ground-floor residents sometimes hung their wet jackets, shoes, or umbrellas there to dry.

The Saha Estates consisted of two buildings: The L-shaped Building A with fourteen units per floor, seven on each wing, and Building B, with seven units per floor, which ran parallel to one leg of Building A, the whole complex forming a U shape. The two buildings were spaced wide apart, but the courtyard in the middle was quite cozy. People referred to the courtyard as the Front Yard. A small playground, a parking lot, the communal faucets, and Granny Konnim's small garden occupied the Front Yard. No child played on the playground; the swing sets and seesaws were so rusted through, they were porous as termite-infested wood. And the parking lot was always empty because no one could afford—or even drive—a car. The only space the residents got good use out of was the garden.

Paint peeled on the outside walls of the buildings, revealing a crack that ran long and deep. The iron railings on every floor were rusted and eroded, leaving rings of brown on the ground where water slid down and pooled on the bottom. The emergency stairs on the sides of the buildings were so rundown one could hardly scale them, so that egress was blocked. Collapsing onto themselves by imperceptible increments, the old buildings exuded dust. And in these buildings, the Sahas ate, slept, and grew old.

The stone pillar at the front gate that bore the name of Saha Estates also had a diagonal crack running through it. The words "Saha" and "Estates," engraved and painted green, were divided by the crack. Saha / Estates. Saha. Estates. Resting against "Saha" was a stack of large black garbage bags that lay like wild animal carcasses, with yellow streaks of rot spilling from them.

The government did not collect garbage at Saha Estates. A contracted company was paid to dispose of the waste, and every so often its representatives expressed their resentment over the small fee Saha residents could afford. On the bulletin board by the custodian's office, they would post a passive-aggressive notice asking residents to reduce waste. And sometimes they would go further, advising them to keep their doors locked, to keep their units sanitary, to refrain from bringing outsiders onto the premises, and so on. The Sahas had no luxury or reason to heed such sound advice.

ONE SPRING DAY, when the bomdong flowers had come in earlier than usual, Granny Konnim sat crouching in her garden with one trowel in hand and a second in her back pocket.

The yellow flower buds reminded Jin-kyung of freesia. She picked a few and made a bouquet. Granny Konnim watched her without a word. She never said anything to anyone if they weeded, picked flowers, or harvested fruits and vegetables in her garden.

Boomboomboomboomboom. Jin-kyung knew without looking back that Woomi was approaching. Footsteps only Woomi's large yet supple frame could make. Of all the people Jin-kyung had ever seen, Woomi was the tallest, had the largest head, the broadest shoulders, thickest knuckles, and knobbiest knees. With that frighteningly enormous body, Woomi always moved quickly, as if flying.

Woomi plopped down next to Jin-kyung as she worked on her bouquet. Jin-kyung said bomdong gets too tough to eat once the flowers come out, and that the flowers taste good fried, but she should watch out for bees hiding in the blossoms—and spoke also of other things of no consequence. Just then, something like a yellow piece of paper flew over and alighted on a flower Jin-kyung was holding.

"Oh, a butterfly!" Jin-kyung exclaimed under her breath.

A yellow more vivid than the blossom. Black whirls like a pair of eyes on the open wings. Feelers growing wide and tapering off at the tips, as if the insect were wearing the feathers of a tiny bird on its head.

"Pretty," said Jin-kyung. "But they say ornate butterflies are poisonous."

Woomi shook her head. "It's a moth," she said, her gaze fixed on the winged insect.

"Butterflies fold their wings when they alight. Moths keep them open. Butterflies have slender feelers with rounded tips, whereas moth feelers are feathery and shaped like leaves. As for poison—who knows? Maybe this fella's poisonous, too."

The yellow butterfly or moth flapped its wings again and flew away.

Born and raised in the Saha Estates, Woomi wasn't able to receive formal education, but her head was an encyclopedia of information no matter the field. A pathological reader especially well versed in history and philosophy, she could also recite quotes from novels and poetry by heart.

Knowing Woomi was probably right, Jin-kyung added anyway, wanting to make this conversation last, "I thought it was too pretty to be a moth."

Woomi curled one corner of her lip into a smirk. "Classification of species by prettiness? That's funny."

Woomi got up and went over to the faucets before Jin-kyung could get in another word.

Set in a hastily cemented cylindrical structure, the eight faucets around the circumference were the only sources of water in the Saha Estates. Saha residents fetched water from these faucets to drink, wash, and do laundry. Accustomed to fetching water on their way back home, no one complained. There was a row of large plastic water jugs and hand carts that the residents used, returned, and kept clean.

Woomi didn't seem to notice the water overflowing. She was staring off with her left eye squinting, as if she'd bit into something sour. She let more water overflow onto the ground than was in the plastic jug, snapped back to reality, and turned off the tap. The old, rusty tap screeched in protest. Woomi would often space out, turn a tap too hard, and twist the han-

dle clean off. Each time the old man had to change out a broken tap, he cackled without a hint of annoyance on his face
and made fun of Woomi.

"Control your strength. Twist gently, like you're handling
a lady."

"A regular joker, aren't you? How about I gently twist
your head off, too?"

Woomi broke things without meaning to. But she never
panicked or apologized, and the old man was always all smiles
even though Woomi put him in his place. Clean, clear lines
appeared at each corner of the old man's mouth when he
smiled.

Woomi stacked three water jugs precariously in a hand
cart, picked up another jug with her free hand, and pushed
the cart coolly toward Building A. The bumpy, steep ramp
that took up the left half of the steps was halfheartedly put
together with cement. Woomi swiftly climbed the ramp, careful to keep the cart balanced.

Jin-kyung still had the bouquet of bomdong in her hand.

Granny Konnim clapped Jin-kyung on the shoulder.
"Didn't get to give her the bouquet, huh?"

Jin-kyung blushed.

Leaning against the railing on the second floor, watching
everything unfurl in the yard, Sara couldn't see the expression
on Jin-kyung's face, but she could see her cheeks flush. She
went downstairs in quick steps.

Sara opened her big eye, the only one she had, widely and
said, "Pretty flowers, Jin-kyung."

Jin-kyung studied the bouquet with uncertainty.

"Who's it for?"

"No one."

Sara kept looking at Jin-kyung, who looked back at her obliviously.

Sara snickered, half-frustrated and half-disappointed, then asked, "Then can I have it?"

Only then did Jin-kyung offer her the bouquet. As Sara received it with both hands and filled her lungs with its fragrance, Jin-kyung walked off toward the stairwell. She'd been thinking about the butterfly the whole time.

"Thanks, Jin-kyung!" Sara shouted.

"What?"

"Thanks for the flowers. Thanks for making me the bouquet?"

Jin-kyung, still entranced, raised her arm and waved at Sara, who lit up with a smile and waved the bouquet in a big arc over her head.

JIN-KYUNG, UNIT 701

Jin-kyung ended up at the park. She couldn't not go. Perhaps because of the late hour, there was nothing there but flimsy police tape—no police, no curious bystanders, or even people out walking. Not even the car where the body was reportedly found. About halfway up the hill, she came across a young couple in school uniforms. They wrapped their arms around each other's waists and kissed, conscious of their audience, then threw a glance at Jin-kyung and giggled to themselves.

When Jin-kyung reached the top of the steps, which were formed naturally with tree roots and earth, a small clearing of about eight square meters appeared. She stood on the edge of the clearing and looked down at the Saha Estates, just across the road from the park.

Though Saha Estates was markedly darker than other parts of Town at night, the smooth solar panels on the roofs caught the moonlight, and murky lights shone from a window here and there. Do-kyung must have stood here once and looked down at their home. *I wonder what went through his mind. Where is he now?* Jin-kyung shut her eyes tight, opened them again, and hurriedly made her way down. She picked up speed, lost her footing and slipped several times. Branches reached out their long arms and scratched her face.

Standing on the side of the four-lane road, Jin-kyung wiped the blood on her cheeks with the back of her hand. Parched, dizzy, and a bit numb, she stepped onto the road. A car racing toward her with awful speed beeped loud and long, swerving into the next lane to avoid her. She stumbled back and collapsed on the sidewalk. A chill started on her crown and made its way down her spine. When they were children, Do-kyung had waited at school, at the empty lot, at the playground for Jin-kyung, who was often late even though she knew he was by himself. In the passing wind, Jin-kyung could almost catch the sound of Do-kyung, a boy crying for his big sister.

Jin-kyung got up, stood with her feet together, and hopped in place three times. One, two, three. She gathered herself, looked both ways, then dashed across the road. And kept running. She went where her legs carried her, thoughtlessly, and eventually found herself back at Saha Estates.

IT WAS ONE night a year ago that Jin-kyung saw Su for the second time. Jin-kyung had been looking up at the sky beyond the railing and pacing the walkway. She walked from Unit 701 to 714 as she smoked, but couldn't see the moon from any spot. Was it hiding behind the clouds? Or was it a new moon? She drew a calendar in her head, filled it with dates, and was calculating the moon cycle when she saw something moving in the distance below. It was too quiet around Saha on that unusually dark night, and two shadowy figures in the deserted yard joined, separated, joined again, and quickly moved past the custodian's office, where the lights were out.

The figures slipped into Building A. One came out and headed across the yard, but spun around halfway and ran back. Jin-kyung ducked, extinguished the cigarette under the heel of her sneaker, and watched the figures in the dark. She could tell who one of the shadows was. She had an ominous feeling that this life and routine she fought to establish—this frail peace—was about to shatter. Jin-kyung plopped to the floor. A crack in the concrete wall ran from ceiling to floor.

Footsteps came up the stairs. *Tatatatap. Tatatatap. Tatatatap.* Just one pair of feet. Footsteps, silence. Footsteps, another stretch of silence. The figure coming up the stairs was running up a floor, stopping at the railing to wave at the figure in the yard. Another floor, more waving. The next floor, waving. The footsteps grew closer until the figure appeared by the seventh-floor stairwell. Someone Jin-kyung knew well: Do-kyung.

Do-kyung went up to the railing in great strides, leaned so far out over he seemed ready to jump, and waved his arms again. Long arms drew great swoops like rainbows in the dark sky. He made other peculiar gestures, then pushed the air with the back of his hand as if to say, *Go, go.* Another gesture at the railing, another look, another gesture. After several rounds of watching and gesturing, he headed down the walkway toward where Jin-kyung was crouching. Unaware his big sister was sitting at the end of the walkway, he quietly hummed a little tune to himself. A voice too hoarse for such a fast, jaunty tune. His raspy voice brought tears to her eyes. When Jin-kyung finally sniffled to stop her nose from dripping, the gentle humming echoing down the walkway stopped.

"Sis?"

"Who was that?"

Do-kyung didn't reply.

"The Town woman?" Jin-kyung asked.

Do-kyung didn't reply.

"Pretty."

Do-kyung was quiet for a long time.

"You saw her?" he finally asked.

Yes, I saw her. The woman who casually frequents this place that must seem scary to Town residents. The woman who keeps running back to you. Who waits for as long as she can to get another look at your small shadow. Who makes you hum melancholy tunes. How could a woman like that not seem pretty in my eyes?

"Yeah."

Do-kyung gave Jin-kyung a sideways glance. "So, you don't . . . remember her?"

Jin-kyung thought of the shadow running across the yard. Small frame. Ponytail bouncing behind her head. Gentle footsteps. One face came to mind. There was a time when Do-kyung was badly scratched on a steel bar at the construction site where he worked. He said he'd picked up disinfectant and bandages at the supermarket and gave himself first aid, but the expert bandaging was telling. Jin-kyung pressed him and Do-kyung said Granny Konnim had helped him. When Jin-kyung thanked Granny Konnim the next day, Granny was surprised.

"Do-kyung got hurt?"

That woman had come to mind then, too.

"Don't worry, sis." Do-kyung extended his hand down to Jin-kyung, who was hunched in silence.

She grabbed his hand and pulled herself up. "You should give her a call later. Being out at this hour . . . she may not say as much, but she'll have been scared."

Do-kyung wrapped an arm around Jin-kyung's shoulders as she turned the doorknob.

"Thanks, sis."

Jin-kyung took another look at the yard where the figure had disappeared.

Inside the apartment, the siblings closed the sliding door to the large room they used as a living room/bedroom and lay down side by side. There was a small extra bedroom in the unit, but they had slept together on a mat in the big bedroom from the very first day they unpacked at Saha. Grown-up siblings did not commonly sleep in the same room, but it was no problem for Jin-kyung and Do-kyung. A grotesque mural etched by rainwater over many years filled the ceiling above them.

All empty units were up for grabs. There was no reason to live on the top floor in a building without an elevator, a floor that was boiling hot in the summer and freezing in the winter. But Jin-kyung went for the unit at the end of the walkway of the top floor as if she wanted things to be as inconvenient as possible. Winters were not so bad. It was cold because there was no heat, but it wasn't dry and there was no condensation in their unit. The summers were a problem, though; the ceiling leaked.

In their second summer in the Saha Estates, it poured every day and flooded all of Granny Konnim's gardens. Water started trickling down one corner of the big bedroom on the veranda side, then advanced bit by bit and took over an entire wall. Water seeped through the ceiling in various places, turned to drops, and dripped from the ceiling. When the uncommonly long monsoon came to an end, mold blossomed along the water stains. Do-kyung was aghast and suggested they move to a different unit. But whatever the reason, Jin-kyung didn't want to.

"We've already spent a year here. Moving from unit to unit is just not . . ."

Wallpaper was stripped off, the walls dried, and the mold on the ceiling was carefully wiped down with diluted bleach. Everything was coated with waterproof paint, but when the following summer rolled around and the monsoon came, the ceiling and walls sprang water stains again. All it took was a little shower. The rainwater cascaded along the water stains of the previous summer and formed new patterns. And so it went: the ceiling was soaked in the monsoon, dried bit by bit for the rest of the year, was soaked again in the next monsoon, then dried again.

Jin-kyung and Do-kyung lay counting the age rings of the water stains above. Do-kyung said he didn't understand why Jin-kyung insisted on living in a unit where the ceiling leaked, but didn't press her to move or threaten to move out into a unit of his own.

Moonlight streamed in through the open window. Jin-kyung watched the shadows on the ceiling, cast by the railing along the veranda, as they slowly leaned right like clock hands. She thought of the day she received frostbite treatment from Su.

Do-kyung nudged her. "Sis?"

Jin-kyung didn't reply. She didn't want him to know she wasn't able to sleep.

"Who are we? We're not mainland people or Town people, so who are we? If we live each day so conscientiously and work hard, what's gonna change? Who'll acknowledge us? Who . . . will . . . forgive me?"

Jin-kyung kept quiet.

Do-kyung let out a deep sigh.

"I want to be a Town Citizen," he added as he rolled over, turning his back to her.

Town Citizen. Citizen.

A month later, Do-kyung and Su made Unit 714 their home.

ON THE NIGHT of Do-kyung's disappearance, Jin-kyung had hardly a wink of sleep all night and just managed to nod off in the morning. A noise as hazy and light as dust settled over her dream. The sounds filtered in like the murmur of the living room TV on weekend mornings from long ago, when she was a little girl, so Jin-kyung thought she was dreaming.

"Hey, HEY! STOP!"

It was the old man's voice. Jin-kyung sprang to her feet. She went out into the walkway and looked down at the yard to find two police buses pulling into the ever-empty parking lot. Granny Konnim, who picked lettuce, cucumbers, and cherry tomatoes in her vegetable patch each dawn, stood by the garden and watched as the old custodian banged on the back end of the bus.

A third of the units at Saha were empty. At first people could just come to Saha and claim a unit. But then some families took up more than one unit or went from unit to unit to avoid cleaning up. Town folk and L2s used Saha as a hideout, and kids up to no good snuck in when the adults weren't looking. When it got to the point where no one knew which units were occupied and which were not, the residents' association decided to put a padlock on every door. The keys to empty units would be kept in a cabinet in the custodian's office, and the residents' representative, Woomi, would keep the cabinet key.

Jin-kyung saw that the police officer speaking with the old man was holding the bundle of keys. The old man and Woomi must have surrendered them. Jin-kyung's hands trembled on the railing. She was about to go back inside and put on some clothes when someone grabbed her shoulder from behind. Jin-kyung reflexively reached around, grabbed the hand on her shoulder, and twisted it behind the person's back. The man screamed, and a young man standing with him aimed a pistol at Jin-kyung's head. The man with the twisted arm, who had unusually white hair, raised his free hand to calm the young man.

"Police," he said to Jin-kyung. "Could you let go?"

The gun aimed at Jin-kyung was lowered as gradually as she backed off. The officer smiled as if he'd expected no less from her and massaged his shoulder.

"You're the sister?"

Jin-kyung didn't answer. There was no reason she should speak or act carelessly without knowing what they knew.

"Su—do you know her?"

Jin-kyung shook her head.

The officer pulled out a photograph from his notepad. "She came around to treat children and such. Oh, I guess you wouldn't know because you don't have any children. But you've heard of her? She's the doctor from the pediatrician's office down the street?"

Jin-kyung shook her head again.

The officer moved his index finger to the corner of his lips, then to his ear. "Are . . . you . . . mute . . . ?"

"No."

"So why don't you speak? I thought you couldn't speak. Let's talk inside. I have the warrant here."

While the white-head took his time unfolding a document, the young officer went ahead inside the apartment. Jin-kyung quickly followed him inside without even taking off her shoes; the older man gripped Jin-kyung's shoulder again.

"The female doctor who died in the park—your brother bothered her . . . well, 'stalked,' based on the word going around. Lots of witnesses who saw them together. I hear that's why she quit the pediatrician's office. So where is he?"

"Don't know. We're not that close."

The officer nodded as if to say, *That happens.* "When'd he go out?"

"I haven't seen him today. We have our own lives now."

"The door to his place is locked. Do you have a spare key?"

"No."

The officer continued to press her on details about Do-kyung even though she kept saying she didn't know. Jin-kyung tried hard to keep a cool head lest she blurt something out. Eventually, the young officer came out of Jin-kyung's apartment, shoving her aside. In his left hand was a plastic bag that contained an old toothbrush, a comb, and an old razor of Do-kyung's. Jin-kyung bit down on her lower lip to stop herself from screaming. The white-head patted her on the shoulder with pity on his face and left.

Do-kyung stalked her. "Stalker, stalker, stalker," she mumbled to herself, the sinister consonants rolling on her tongue.

JIN-KYUNG AND DO-KYUNG had come to the Saha Estates three years earlier.

Stumbling home drunk as always, their father had been mugged one night, beaten to within an inch of his life. After the attack, he could manage no more than breathing. Jin-kyung's mother, who'd run away from her husband twice, returned to nurse her bedridden husband and provided for the family with unbelievable devotion.

Every house has its own unique atmosphere. The atmosphere in Jin-kyung's came from her father lying like a corpse, nails sticking out of the wall at inexplicable places and angles, a blinking halogen light, cobwebs in every corner of the ceiling, and an empty fridge. One day, Jin-kyung couldn't take that languid, muted atmosphere anymore and said she wished he would die already.

Mother was not surprised or angry. Indifferently, she asked why that was.

"Like it's never crossed your mind," Jin-kyung said.

"No," she said. "I hope he goes on like this forever."

"Why?"

"Because it is now my role to look after your father. And to begrudge and curse this man who cannot speak a word, let alone get up. This is all I am. I am nothing without your father."

Each time Mother inserted the suction tube into the small opening of Father's trachea, his eyes flew open and his stiff board of a body jerked as if to prove he was still a living thing.

Mother hummed quietly while she tended to him. *Mea culpa. I kneel before my lord. Forgive us our sins. Deliver us from evil.* Mother wasn't religious, but she'd heard a lot of hymns at her Catholic high school. As she sat Father up and patted him on the back, washed him, and sanitized the medical devices hooked up to various parts of his body, Jin-kyung wanted to ask, *What on earth is your sin? Why are you kneeling? What have you done that needs forgiving?*

Six years he lived on. He died the spring Jin-kyung turned seventeen.

At the time, Mother worked for a moving company, packing and unpacking kitchenware and children's clothes and toys. On the day after Father's funeral, she left the house at seven in the morning as usual, packed for a small family with a lot of books and toys, and moved them into a house with a big yard. She wrapped every fragile item with bubble wrap, carefully fit them into boxes, loaded them onto a truck, traveled two hours to the new home, put everything in its right place, cleaned up, and got home after her own children had eaten ramen for dinner. The morning after that, and the morning after that, Mother told Jin-kyung to take good care of her little brother before heading off to work.

Her last morning was no different. As Jin-kyung walked her to the door, Mother warmly patted her shoulder and said, "I'm off." That was it. She looked the way she looked every morning; she didn't pause or glance back as she stepped over the threshold. Her coworkers at the moving company said the same thing at the wake. She was her usual self that day. She got herself a second coffee halfway through the shift, saying she was tired; she hummed a tune all day long, and cleaned her plate at lunch. She put the laundry basket and detergent away by the washing machine in the veranda of their client's new apartment, and then fell out the window to the flower bed ten stories below.

The wake was sparsely attended. Exhausted from just getting by, Jin-kyung's mother couldn't hang on to relationships. The only blood relation she had remained in contact with, other than her children, was her eldest sister, but Jin-kyung didn't know her phone number. She had no friends to speak of. Very few relatives on her father's side showed up, perhaps thinking they'd fulfilled their share of family duty by attending his funeral just four months before. Father's younger brother came alone, drank for a while, and left without a word. A cousin came to deliver a condolence envelope on behalf of Father's older brother.

To Jin-kyung's surprise, Mother's coworkers at the moving company were the ones who wept. They were middle-age men who had only ever interacted with Mother while working. Strenuous work, the sudden death, and the police investigation that followed had left them tense and unnerved, triggering the burst of tears. Maybe they were more afraid than sad. It could have been one of them that fell, and their children were as young and frail as Jin-kyung and Do-kyung—this made them feel scared and helpless.

The men held Jin-kyung and Do-kyung's bony hands for an uncharacteristically long time. The owner of the moving company—who, as the last witness, came to the funeral straight from the police station—had claimed Mother's death was a suicide, not an accident. When he politely said that her death was a great loss to the company, but mourning was all he would do for her, the coworkers furtively let go of the children's hands.

The men stayed up at the wake. They didn't play cards or drink or eat, but sat around in silence, and took turns lighting a new incense stick when the old one was about to burn out. Like faint proof that Mother had once lived, a thread of smoke rose from the incense and dissolved in the air. Her funerary shrine would have been empty but for the bitter, sharp smoke.

Jin-kyung sat lopsided, not even leaning against a wall,

alternately crying and nodding off. Someone was singing. *Mea culpa. I kneel before my lord. Forgive us our sins. Deliver us from evil.* Jin-kyung felt the orientation of her soul turn inside out. She went blind, as if her optic nerves had been severed. The mysterious ringing in her ears that drowned out everything slowly subsided and she could hear shouting, screaming, and Do-kyung crying. For the first and last time in Jin-kyung's life, she hit Do-kyung. She hit him so hard he couldn't close his eyes or mouth, and only when Do-kyung spat out a broken tooth did she manage to stop punching him.

From that day on, Do-kyung became inseparable from Jin-kyung. It seemed at first glance that a boy who'd lost both parents was clinging to his only remaining family, but how Do-kyung felt wasn't as simple as that.

Jin-kyung quit school and pumped gas by day, waited tables in the evening, and worked graveyard shifts at the convenience store. One morning, weighed down by exhaustion, she came home and realized her toothbrush was missing. She hadn't thought much of it then. But the next week, when her replacement toothbrush disappeared, she asked Do-kyung about it. He said he didn't know. About a month later, when the toothbrush was gone again, she yelled at Do-kyung: "Did you throw it out? Did you drop it in the toilet? How come we put our toothbrush in the same holder and mine always goes missing?" Do-kyung was clearly rattled that Jin-kyung yelled at him, and she apologized.

After Do-kyung went to school, Jin-kyung turned the house inside out. She looked in the trash, the shoe closet, and every corner of the fridge, but couldn't find her toothbrush.

She was about to give up and get dressed for work when an old tin pencil case sitting on Do-kyung's floor table caught her eye. No way. Dented and warped, the pencil case had to be pried open, and when it was, toothbrushes with yellowing bristles popped out, scattering on the table. They were all Jin-kyung's. One was very worn, and the other three were very new.

"In case you ran away," Do-kyung explained.

Jin-kyung cornered him, scolding him, but all Do-kyung could do was shake his head and cry.

"Speak up! Why would I run away? Where would I go? How does hiding my toothbrush change anything?"

"I don't know."

Jin-kyung stopped pressing. She knew he was telling the truth.

THE OWNER DIDN'T recognize Do-kyung at first. In order to meet him face-to-face, Do-kyung had submitted a résumé to the moving company, and even passed an interview with the supervisor—all simply for the opportunity to get the owner alone.

"My mother didn't kill herself."

This was the only thing Do-kyung said to the owner in his small office. "Huh? What? What's wrong with you?" the owner asked repeatedly, and got the same answer every time: "My mother didn't kill herself." Placing his hands on the corners of the well-worn wooden desk, he got up with a flummoxed look on his face and shuddered as if a chill swept over him. He slowly examined Do-kyung's right eye, then left, then his nose, philtrum, the curve of his top lip, and the corners of his mouth, and said, "Your mother killed herself."

"My mother! Didn't kill herself!"

"Your mother killed herself. And she left an unbelievable mess by jumping off the veranda of a client's new home, for crying out loud. The railing came up past her waist. There's no way she lost her balance and fell over."

Do-kyung repeated himself and the owner shook his head as if he'd had enough. He rose to his feet, but didn't manage to take a single step. Do-kyung had driven a box cutter into the owner's side.

Do-kyung climbed on top of the owner and with a single cry stabbed him four more times around the shoulders and solar plexus. He lodged the box cutter in the man's throat, and ran away.

The sight of her brother covered in blood and shivering brought to mind the old Estates over in Town. Jin-kyung thought of the small Town-country somewhere down south that had become independent decades ago. The country that built a tall, impenetrable wall between it and the rest of the world. And the Saha Estates was a secluded island within the isolated country. Where in the world could they find a more perfect hideout? Jin-kyung knew they would never be caught, if only they could get there. Assuming the place actually existed.

The siblings stole into a cargo ship and crossed the ocean. When the ship docked at Town's harbor, they jumped into the water not knowing if they'd ever get out again, and hid there until the sun went down. In the early spring chill, they swam across the night sea, racing with the wind in their faces. Saha Estates—it was real.

When Jin-kyung and Do-kyung arrived at the custodian's office with a thin crust of frost on their faces, Do-kyung crashed to the floor, and Jin-kyung wanted to say, *Help us. Save us*, but her lips would not move at all. The old man took the siblings to his own apartment, which was attached to the office. He fetched warm water from the control room, filled his tub with it, stripped them down to their underwear, and had them soak.

Covering their heads with a towel he'd dipped in the water, he said to Jin-kyung, "Keep soaking the towel so it doesn't get cold. Warm your face first. It's gonna hurt. Hang in there. And don't slip away. You've come this far. It'll be a shame to let go now."

Jin-kyung warmed Do-kyung's face with the wet towel and repeated the old man's words: "Don't slip away. You've come this far. It'll be a shame to let go now."

Do-kyung gritted his teeth and nodded.

AFTER A LONG residents' meeting, the Saha Estates decided to accept Jin-kyung and Do-kyung into their midst. They were the first complete outsiders—not L2s who lost their citizenship, or natives and their children who couldn't get L2 status—since the old man, who had arrived ten years prior.

"Seems unfitting to welcome or congratulate you," the old man said as he handed Jin-kyung a key with a sympathetic look, as if he were comforting a pair of rejects. "Just be glad you made it."

Jin-kyung cleared most of the trash from their unit and went to the temp agency as the old man had instructed. He'd said that was the first thing she had to do if she wanted to live in Town. One needed money to live, and a job to make that money, but the Sahas couldn't get jobs by submitting résumés and going on interviews like others.

The temp agency was in an office building not far from Saha. An endless stream of office workers in snappy clothes shuffled in and out of the revolving front doors. Jin-kyung went around the back as the old man had told her. Next to the parking garage ramp was a small door without a sign that led to a narrow hall with a low ceiling, which led to another small metal door, also without a sign. She opened the door. A two-seater sofa worn shiny sat facing her, and next to it was a large, sturdy old desk and chair.

The agent was sitting at the desk clipping her nails. There was tissue paper spread in front of her, but the nails flew every-where. She was an old lady in a plain sweater and wool pants. Her lips were painted deep red and she wore her short gray hair in very tight curls. In some ways she looked like any other old woman her age, and in other ways she looked out of her mind. She bore a very conspicuous scar right under her eye; about an inch long, it looked like she'd been stabbed hard with a blade. It seemed the wound hadn't been treated properly when she was injured, as the scar had healed grotesquely, some parts sunk in, other parts bubbled up, and the skin around it discolored.

She had to be at least eighty. She moved clumsily, spoke in a drawl, had a slight tremor. Holding a luxury fountain pen in her trembling hand, she filled in the form herself.

"Building and unit?"

"Building A, Unit 701."

"The hardest to get to and the coldest. Age?"

"Thirty. I'm thirty. My brother's . . . twenty-five."

"What did you do before?"

"I waited tables and stuff. My brother was in school."

The agent looked Jin-kyung up and down, nodded slowly, and told her that she'd contact her through the custodian if work came in.

Tight rows of magnolia trees lined her way back to Saha. Dry branches bore ivory buds soft as expensive tissues. The sun was setting, dyeing the magnolia buds red, and flags hanging between the trees in long intervals flapped languidly. On each of the flags was a figure: a star with seven points. She'd seen that symbol before, framed and hung at the front of the office building where the temp agency was.

Back at Saha, Jin-kyung stopped by the custodian's office to ask about the national flag.

"National flag?" the old man said, looking at her sideways with his bottom lip pouting. "I suppose a madcap country like this could have a national flag, but I don't remember seeing one. Are you talking about the heptagram? That's the insignia of the Council of Ministers."

Below the custodian's office window was a long wooden desk with many grooves on the surface, and hidden below that was a safe. The old man sat on a wheeled chair that was set far too low for the height of the desk, next to a small refrigerator. The space was perfect for a maximum capacity of one.

Jin-kyung became a frequent visitor at the tiny office even

though the old man was demonstratively annoyed by it. She sat on the desk or leaned against the armrest of the chair, and sometimes settled on the floor. Having grown up with a father who was immobile in his final years, and a mother who never expressed herself, Jin-kyung had little experience with adults, and typically felt uncomfortable around the elderly. But she was drawn to the old custodian. He liked to talk, mostly to berate someone or lament or be defeatist in the extreme, but there was just something about him that put people at ease. Each time Jin-kyung barged in without so much as a knock on the door, he would grumble and hand her the folding chair from the corner.

One day that first month, Jin-kyung was in the custodian's office dusting the folding chair when the jingle for the TV news came on the custodian's small television. The old man stretched his arm toward the TV and turned it up. Jin-kyung marveled at the fact that the television had no channel knob, since there was only one channel.

"This is an idiot box," the old man said, his eyes fixed on the screen. "This turns people into real idiots. Best not to watch."

The daily report of the spokesperson for the Council of Ministers began. The report always came on before the daily news to share with Town Citizens the Council's decisions, opinions, and progress with government projects: *Medical insurance coverage will be expanded and partial adjustment of premiums announced, private child-care centers will enter gradual municipalization, and Residential District 3 ownership will be transferred to the state.* The spokesperson continued, "Several branches of the research center run by the National Hospital were bought out by the largest medical foundation in the world, and the Ministry of Means and Industry is to be removed from the government branch and reestablished as a public corporation."

"That's nice," said Jin-kyung. "They must be happy, Town people."

The old man laughed bitterly. "This is a huge corporation. A corporation called 'public' fattening itself. People with no money can't go to the hospital or have children, but all the public organizations that churn out money are practically owned by a select few."

Looking at the insignia on the spokesperson's podium, Jin-kyung thought about the flags flapping in the streets. She hardly ever saw the national flag in the country she had fled from. This was a country that flew the flag of a Council of Ministers, not even the national flag, in the streets. Where a Council pronounced its decisions every day, and the people mistook this one-sided report for communication.

The Council report ended and the news began, and the old man turned off the TV.

"Astounding, isn't it?" said the old man. "Why does Town even let the Sahas live in the Saha Estates?"

"I guess it was decided. By the Council."

"And why did the Council come to that decision?"

Jin-kyung looked blankly at the old man's reflection on the dark TV screen, sensing that he wasn't looking for an answer.

"Did Town people decide on it?" the old man muttered as if to himself.

Jin-kyung and the old man's eyes met through their reflections. The old man was not smiling.

IN JIN-KYUNG'S FIRST year at Saha Estates, summer began with a vengeance, with fire. The oppressive sun during the day was tolerable compared to the suffocating heat wave that raged under the moon. Exhausted from another tropical night, the old man was nodding off with all the office windows and doors open. He woke up at the slightest hint of cool relief from the fan that kept breathing hot air on him, then fell back asleep again. Half awake, he heard a polite knock on his door. *Knock, knock, knock*. Not too fast, not too slow, perfectly spaced. The old man couldn't get his eyes to open. *Knock, knock, knock*, came the reprise. He could feel someone was blocking the fan, too, but couldn't manage to move.

"Are you all right, sir?" The old man was shaken out of his slumber.

"Sleep paralysis, huh? You're dripping with sweat! And today's not even as hot as yesterday."

The old man was instantly put off. This stranger was condescendingly friendly and accommodating. The old man gave him a blank look that communicated neither thanks nor curiosity. The man pulled out an ID from his back pocket. Cop.

"There was a fire last night. The intersection downtown. You hear anything about it?"

"No, I didn't hear anything about it, asshole."

The cop laughed. Then he dragged a chair from outside the office, sat down in front of the old man, and looked him in the eye.

"Someone burned the heptagram flags. Had the nerve to

set them all on fire from the downtown center all the way to the Parliament. Luckily the fires didn't spread and we put them out, but the arsonist's gone. See anyone suspicious around three in the morning?"

This was routine. Crimes against no one in particular and therefore difficult to narrow down suspects always sent at least one cop to the Saha Estates, no matter where the crime took place.

"Don't know," the old man said, waving him off. "Someone sets fire downtown and you come looking for him here?"

A man in his forties who lived on the second floor of Building A walked in through the main gate, yawning lazily. Eyes not completely open, he nodded in the direction of the office to greet the old man. As he languidly climbed the stairs, the cop followed him with his gaze.

"That man—he's coming back just now?"

"Cleans the roads at night. The guy you're looking for isn't here. I guarantee you. So don't come poking around and wasting your time whenever something's up. Go look downtown."

"Oh, you *guarantee*? Knowing their stunning pasts?"

Small squabbles often took place at Saha. Sometimes residents were arrested for assaulting a Citizen or causing a disturbance, usually over unsettled pay. The case generally closed with the Saha resident not getting the compensation or medical treatment they were promised. A life of doing repetitive menial labor without any assurance of compensation was like walking down a path backward. Life was terrifying and tedious. Each time they paused to take stock of their lives, they found themselves unfailingly worse off than before; Saha residents thus grew more childish, petty, and simpleminded.

The following morning, the police took the man on the second floor of Building A, in addition to Jin-kyung, Do-kyung, and two other residents in their twenties down to the precinct for questioning. The real arsonist turned himself in the next day and Jin-kyung was released, but not before receiving a large bruise on her arm. Jin-kyung brushed it off, telling the old man she ran into the door on the bus home.

"What kind of bruise swells up in seconds?" the old man said as he took out a roll-on pain-relief liquid from his desk drawer. *The cops don't know anything about folks at Saha*, he grumbled.

THE ARSONIST WAS, as the old man predicted, an L—a Citizen. A nondescript retiree in his sixties. He was drunk when he committed the crime.

A lifetime public servant, he was spending his retirement volunteering at the info desk at the District Office. He had been known to say controversial things at times. Every chance he got, he'd tell anyone who would listen, be it staff or visitor, that Town was not a real country, that Town took care of its people like wholesale supermarkets kept track of their stock; he'd argue that the anonymous Council of Ministers system must be abolished immediately and that Town should be obligated to join an international organization and follow international laws. He wasn't old or naïve enough for his words to be brushed aside as the mad ramblings of a senile old man. Several complaints from Citizens and warnings from staff only made him more aggressive.

This man had never set foot anywhere else. Born in Town when it was still just a small village by the sea, he spent his school years here, passed the Town Civil Service Exam, got a job, married a Citizen, and made a life here. His strange comments began three years ago, right after his father passed away.

His father had lived long enough and died of liver cancer. Too old and frail for cancer treatment, he wasn't sad or frightened but prepared for the end by controlling the pain with opioids. He arranged for his house, books, and property to be donated, said goodbye to his dear friends and family, cooked for his grandchildren, and recorded the disease's process with photographs and essays to put together the manuscript for *Cancer Grandpa's Kitchen*. Following his granddaughter's advice, he took *Cancer* out of the title. With his dying breath he thanked his daughter-in-law, told his grandson to stay out of trouble, and asked his granddaughter to have his cookbook published. And to his son, he said, "I regret one thing in life, and because of that one thing, I regret my entire life."

No one in his family could have guessed the one regret in his life. Even his son, who admired his father but rarely conversed with him, was in the dark.

After soberly taking care of his father's funeral, the arsonist continued to be his friendly self at the District Office info desk, and started to drink four or five glasses of whiskey every night. His wife thought it was the grief, until he doubled over in the District Office bathroom one night and was taken to the emergency room. When he managed to wake up after two hours, his first words to the doctor were: "If a doctor doesn't treat a sick person, can you still call him a doctor?"

Best-case scenario, he would be charged with arson. If he was found guilty of violating Special Law, there was no telling how heavy a sentence he would receive. Special Law had no standards, grounds, or appeals. His family stressed that he had worked for Town all his life as a public servant, was disabled early in life as a result of an automobile accident at work, was in a state of great shock following his father's death, and had since suffered from depression. As such, his action was perceived as a conscious death wish or the result of an unsound mind.

WHEN JIN-KYUNG CAME by to return the muscle relaxant balm the next day, the old man glanced at her arm. The dark bruise was turning yellow.

"Keep it."

"But it's yours."

"It's got your sweat on it."

"It had your sweat on it to begin with."

"I don't sweat."

Jin-kyung took the cap off the bottle and rubbed her arm in big strokes. The alcohol in the balm cooled her arm as it evaporated.

The television news was reporting on the arson. His eyes glued to the screen, the old man kept muttering the word *lunatic*. The arsonist's features were obscured by a big white mask and baseball cap pulled down over his forehead, but the smooth curve of his jawline was visible. Clean-shaven, white, plump. Telling of the plentiful, stable life he'd led. Jin-kyung rubbed her own chin against her bruised arm. Her skin was as taut and rough as a towel that had been drying in direct sunlight for too long.

"Why throw that all away?" Jin-kyung murmured, and the old man turned off the TV with the remote.

"We have nothing to lose," the old man said after a long silence, the words coming out slowly as if squeezing out from under oppressive thoughts. "So why aren't we doing something like that? The Butterfly Riot was the first and last of its kind."

In the early days of Town, there had been a widespread protest among L2s and Sahas against the new government. Protests, riots, revolution—it had many names now, but the old man called it the Butterfly Riot. Jin-kyung had a feeling the old man had participated in it, too, but couldn't ask.

She thought, *Seriously. Why not? Why aren't we doing something like that?*

ANOTHER DAY, ANOTHER round of unit-by-unit search. The undercover police were becoming lax, wandering around the Saha Estates looking bored. Jin-kyung was staring blankly down at the yard with her hands on the walkway railing. A pair of slender feet with sky-blue nail polish on the big toes came into view beside her. Sara. Sara wrapped her soft, long fingers around Jin-kyung's hand, and Jin-kyung yanked it back with a start. Her heart sank each time she looked at Sara. The white of her eye as white as a glacier, her pupil a depthless twinkling blue. Such a beautiful eye, but only one. It wasn't because of her one-eyedness that Jin-kyung had pulled away, but Sara seemed to think so. Sara took Jin-kyung's hand again.

"Do-kyung is with me."

"What?"

Sara lowered her head and scanned the area once.

"They didn't turn over everything, my place being a single woman's apartment. He was hiding in the refrigerator."

"Everything's fine?"

"Yeah. But it wasn't him. I know. Do-kyung and the doctor came for drinks at the bar where I work."

Jin-kyung felt relief, then was hit by a pang of nerves. *What went through Do-kyung's mind as he hid, contorted in the refrigerator?*

Jin-kyung held Sara's hand.

"From now on, stay away from me," she said to Sara, who held her gaze.

"Jin-kyung, I'm scared, too."

Jin-kyung pulled Sara to the stairwell, where they were hidden from any eyes in the yard, and gave her a warm hug. "Please," she said.

Sara nodded several times before turning and running down the stairs.

She had been born without a right eye. She started wearing an eye patch—two-strap eye band, one strap running over the left eye and the other under—at six and never took it off. When her mother died, she signed a release form to turn her body over to the research center because she couldn't afford a burial. Even then, she held back tears so as not to get her eye patch wet.

Many people showed interest in Sara, both inside and outside Saha, but she spurned their advances. Because of Jin-kyung. But Jin-kyung hadn't been aware of Sara's feelings or even her own as she held her tight and asked her to look after her brother.

SARA, UNIT 214

She never drank while on the clock. But the scent of the cognac lingered at the tip of her nose that day. It was the kind Sara was fond of. Matured in an oak case without caramel or other additives, the cognac was subtly sweet and fruity, good for cocktails. The regulars responded well to her recommendation, and an order had been put in for a few more bottles. She poured the cognac in a tumbler, wet her lips slowly with the tip of her tongue, and took a small sip. Honeyed, crisp flavor filled her mouth. She savored it a little at a time until even she could tell that she'd taken quite a bit from the bottle.

"Something going on?" the bar owner, who'd been pretending not to notice, asked without looking in Sara's direction. Nothing was going on. Sara was thinking how strange it was to feel so nervous and excited when nothing was going on.

Sara laughed to show she was fine and said, "Nothing's going on. Maybe something's about to happen. I hope it's something nice."

"Oh, by the way," her boss said as she reached under the bar shelf for a shopping bag. "I saw it in the window and thought it was pretty and got it for myself, but it's too tight on me. Hard to move around in it. I think it'll fit you. Do you want it? I've had it here since Monday and forgot about it."

It was a dress. The top looked like a blouse that would go with a suit, and the dress came down to the knees. The shoulders were fitted but the rest of the dress flared out and appeared good for a range of sizes. Her boss was slightly taller than her but more or less the same size. Sara knew well why she had bought the dress and was adding these superfluous explanations. Perfume, lipstick, pumps, and bags, all nearly or completely new, were handed down to Sara for similar reasons.

"Thank you. I guess something good was about to happen after all!"

Accepting gifts happily, and not being offended or uneasy. Communicating unambiguous gratitude. This was how Sara responded. She told herself she should wear this dress to work the next day. Feeling even better, she drank another glass of cognac.

She got off work a little early because there were no customers. She thought she'd get a good night's sleep, but it turned out she'd consumed just the right amount of alcohol to keep sleep away. She was restless the entire night. She got up and went over to the refrigerator to knock herself out with more alcohol when the front door rattled. The wind? Moments later, there was a clear knock. Sara froze in front of her refrigerator. *Knock, knock.* She thought she heard someone's voice as well.

She was going to ask, *Who is it?* but changed her mind. "What do you want?"

"Let me in," answered a voice as quiet and fluttering as a gentle wind. It was Do-kyung. Sara quickly crawled over to the door to confirm.

"Who is it?"

"It's Do-kyung."

Jin-kyung's younger brother. Living on the seventh floor with Su. Or were they living together? Technically, Su was just a frequent guest at Do-kyung's place.

WHEN SARA HEARD that siblings of thirty and twenty-five moved into Unit 701, she asked the neighbors if it was true. Twice. The unit was made up of just one tiny bedroom and a living room with a small veranda. Wouldn't they want more space, both brother and sister? Two years later, when Sara heard that Do-kyung was going to live with the doctor who treated the children at Saha Estates, she asked if that was true. Four times.

Town Citizens received medical treatment for free. But the medical insurance fee was so high it was hard to believe it was for a national health plan. Properties were confiscated because of late fees and people filed for bankruptcy or even gave up Citizen status because they couldn't afford the insurance. As it was impossible to see a doctor or get drugs prescribed without an insurance number, the residents of Saha endured all illnesses with the few pain medications they could buy at the supermarket. A scratch from a nail sticking out on the floor or a bug bite could lead to a severe infection. Illness and injury seemed an inescapable destiny.

Children were especially vulnerable. The Department of Public Health made regular visits to Saha to check on the children and give them basic immunization, but that was the extent of it. Unless they came down with an infectious disease that required immediate attention, the children weren't offered treatment. The doctors came and examined them thoroughly, did blood tests, kindly informed the parents what their children were sick with and what the prognosis was, and left. The desperate and heartbreaking cases had no one to turn to but Su.

Sara remembered the first day they came to the bar together. Su pushed the heavy glass door open slowly but with force. She looked around like any other customer and picked the table by the window, everyone's preferred spot, and a man with his head buried in his chest followed her in. Sara recognized his shoes. The material looked like fake leather, but it had aged nicely. They were sneakers with shoelaces, definitely not dressy, but they didn't seem odd. This had left an impression on Sara when she first saw them at Saha, and she often thought of the sneakers whenever Do-kyung came to mind. And now he was here.

The two sat with a small table between them. Do-kyung hung his head so low that Sara wondered, *Do I pretend I don't see him? But I have to get their order, don't I?* Then Do-kyung looked over at Sara and waved with his left hand as if to say, *Hi, it's me!*

Sara took their order and brought them their food and drinks as she would with any other customers. Do-kyung only acknowledged her with a nod and didn't ask after her or introduce Su. Su sat with her upper body sprawled on the table, her head resting on her right outstretched arm, which Do-kyung held from time to time. Do-kyung seemed to be doing most of the talking, while Su listened and sometimes laughed so hard her shoulders shook.

After about the third visit, Su began to acknowledge Sara. Sara would test out a new cocktail on the couple or sit for a while and chat. One time, Su complained about a guy she used to see. He apparently showed up to a date so unprepared that she was the one who had to decide where to go, what to eat, and so on.

Do-kyung teasingly said he could relate to the guy. "You have very strong opinions. Even with us, there are so many things we have to do, places we have to see, things we have to eat—we hardly ever do what I want."

"Are you saying it's my fault?"

"I'm not saying it's a fault. Like today, for instance. It was your idea to come here."

"Oh sure! Whose idea was it to come here the first time? Who said this place was the most relaxing?"

Sara sat between them, not knowing what to do with herself. They continued to argue as if she weren't there, then Do-kyung apologized, held Su's hand, and moved on to another topic. Sara was fascinated by this couple who discussed exes, bickered in her presence, and made up in the time it took to say, "I'm sorry."

Strange couple, Sara thought. *Strange and good together.*

WHEN SARA OPENED the door for Do-kyung that night, he was alone. He asked her to hide him, and Sara didn't ask what for. *Did he kill someone again?* She thought that may be the case, but she wasn't afraid.

YONHWA, BEFORE SHE was Sara's mom, was a native who did not qualify for Citizen status when Town became independent. She'd been twenty at the time. She wasn't a student and didn't have a proper job. She had failed to get into college and was preparing for the college entrance exam a second time while temping here and there to get by—a convenience store in the mornings, a boutique in the afternoons. Passing out over her books night after night, she wanted to cut back on work, but she needed to make some extra money for herself in addition to contributing to her family's expenses. When Town became independent and the Citizenship Application Plan went into effect, she was in an in-between state but working hard each day.

No one in Yonhwa's family qualified for citizenship. Yonhwa's father became an L2, became a two-year contract worker at the distribution company where he worked, and his salary was cut by nearly half. Her father hung on as long as he could, quit the distribution company, and left Town in search of a new job. Yonhwa, who also became L2 and was left in charge of her two young siblings, hung on as long as she could before sending her siblings to a facility. And in the big house that she used to share with her family, Yonhwa lived alone, taking on the rent by herself. She wanted her family to be able to return to this home when she had everything sorted out. But after becoming an L2, Yonhwa kept getting fired from her temp job for incomprehensible reasons, such as not wearing makeup or forgetting to greet her boss first thing when she came to work. For several months, she couldn't make rent. She left the house and moved into the Saha Estates, lost touch with her father, and rarely visited her siblings.

Yonhwa was fired again from a kitchen job at a general hospital, a position she had just barely managed to secure. The reason was that she lived in the Saha Estates—but L2s weren't qualified for a spot in the staff dormitory. The hospital said that she could have her job back as soon as she got a cleaner, safer place to live. But one couldn't find a clean, safe place without a job or money.

No place to go and nothing to do, Yonhwa went down to the Saha yard and sat on the creaking seesaw. When the custodian strolled over and sat across from her, she felt tears spring to her eyes and covered her face with her hands. The seesaw screeched like it was about to snap and instantly tipped to the custodian's side, sending Yonhwa up in the air. The large man, with facial features that tended to defy symmetry and gave off an unsettling impression, smiled at her with an uncharacteristically gentle look.

"There's a temp agency. Across the street in the parking garage of the tallest building."

"Excuse me?"

"The Saha folks usually get work from the agent lady there. It's tough work, so they hire people like us. If you're really desperate, you could try there."

Yonhwa did not nod, even though she knew she was going to try the agency.

From that day on, Yonhwa worked wherever the agent lady sent her. Sometimes she lasted a day, most frequently a week, and other times months. The job was usually to count stock, wrap things, unwrap things, tidy up, clean, sanitize, or throw things out. Every once in a while, she put on pretty clothes to solicit visitors at fairs or store openings. The work was easier and the hourly pay was better, but these were onetime jobs that only lasted a few hours and didn't amount to much money.

The work got harder as time went on, she was unable to save up, and it seemed unlikely that she would be able to bring her family back together. Yonhwa had planned to work hard, become financially capable, learn a skill and get a license in it, and eventually become a Citizen. She was going to find her father and get her siblings back from the facility. But working day and night didn't increase her bank balance, and the work she could get was menial and had nothing to do with qualifications or skills. She was stuck in the same life as she extended her L2 status, and it seemed she would soon lose her L2 status, too, unless something changed.

Eventually, thoughts of her family no longer brought up any tenderness in her. Resentment toward her father, and the burden of looking after her siblings, and the guilt of having sent them away, deepened. She didn't excel at anything, nor did she work herself to death, but she had applied herself in earnest. Didn't she deserve something a little better than the edge of a cliff at the end of the world? Yonhwa was sick of the whole thing.

One evening a few days before Christmas, Yonhwa was buried under the covers in her bed at home after two hours of soliciting customers in a short skirt outside a restaurant's grand opening. Winter was particularly cold, and it had been overcast since morning, as if it might start snowing any minute. Yonhwa shivered. As she warmed under the covers, she realized that it might be a white Christmas and she couldn't care less. She was nearly asleep when someone banged on her door. It was the custodian. Without opening the door or crawling out from under the blankets, Yonhwa asked him what he wanted. He replied that she had an urgent call from the temp agency.

The agent told her over the phone in the custodian's office that there was a kitchen position at a big Christmas party the very next day. Yonhwa had apparently worked for them before, and the catering service had asked for Yonhwa specifically.

"Why me specifically?" she asked.

"How should I know?" said the agent. "It's not like you're good with your hands. I suppose they liked you. Who knows what employers are looking for?"

Yonhwa suddenly felt like giving up on everything. So she said no. No, she would not be taking this job or any other job, so please never contact her again.

"What's your plan?" The agent laughed incredulously. "Starve to death?"

"I'd rather starve to death. None of the jobs you find me ever get me anywhere, no matter how hard I work. I only get more sick. So unless you have a life-changing job for me, don't call me."

Yonhwa hung up. As she made her way up the stairs, she thought that she didn't care if she starved or got sick to death. Back under the warm covers, she was instantly in heaven.

THE AGENT GOT Yonhwa a life-changing job after all. Marriage. With a Citizen. Most women could marry a Citizen and receive citizenship with their husband's sponsorship. Sponsoring a native woman through marriage was the last resort for Town men who wanted a wife. As Citizens, none of these men were financially or socially lacking. Most of them were too old, calamitously flawed in their appearance or health, or seeking a vastly abnormal family culture, living environment, or marriage arrangement. The brokers sugarcoated the truth about the men by saying they were too focused on their careers, too shy to ask women out, and so forth, but truthfully, none of them were like that.

Yonhwa's suitor was old. Sixty-eight. He had been widowed a year prior, and had a son who was married and not on good terms with him.

The agent showed Yonhwa a picture that seemed at least ten years old. "I'm not so sure about this, either, but I figured I'd ask, since you wanted 'life-changing.' He's richer than anything. He lives in Royal Estates by himself. He says he isn't leaving a thing to his son when he dies. He wants to live out the rest of his life with a nice, obedient woman and leave her everything. I've met him, and he seems normal. He may not be that normal given that he's looking for someone as young as you, but that's neither here nor there. I'm willing to go with you as witness at the ceremony and vouch for your character. Well? You want to go live with him?"

"I have to decide if I want to marry him now? I don't get to meet him first?"

"You want to meet him first? Go out to dinner and a movie? Hold hands for the first time? You want to date this guy? He's gonna keel over and die waiting for you to make up your mind. Just think of the money. Don't think about anything else and just tell me right now—live with him, yes or no? What do you want to meet with him for? It's not like you're gonna fall in love with a man approaching seventy."

Yonhwa thought about her own father. He was in his fifties. People of his generation married younger, so if her grandfather were alive, he would be . . . eighty?

Watching Yonhwa calculate the three men's ages with her

fingers, the agent said, "Don't think about how much older or younger he is than your father and your grandfather! It's not like they're ever going to meet. All it does is make you feel worse."

This is probably about as life-changing as it gets, Yonhwa thought. She considered for a moment and said, "Worst-case scenario?"

"Worst? He kills you," said the agent. "But he made all his money legally by investing. He's not the kind to get entangled with shady types."

"How about worst-*possible*-case scenario?"

"You hate it. You hate living with the old man. The more he likes you and paws you, the more your skin crawls, you're disgusted. If you hate it so much, you can always run away. Won't be my problem. I won't hide you, but I won't blame you, either. But then you'll end up a Saha, not even the L2 you are now."

Yonhwa agreed to marry him. The worst imaginable case wasn't worse than where she was at the moment. Looking back, she saw that she'd never made a choice in her life that yielded the most gain. She'd always made a balance sheet of losses and opted for losing less. In any case, she alone suffered the consequences of her own choices.

IT WAS NOTHING like the agent had predicted. At first the old husband loved his young wife. He loved her so much. Yonhwa lived in a house overflowing with sunlight, ate flavorful meals, wore clothes made of soft fabric, and slept under white sheets. But she had to wipe the streaks and stains off the windows every day, bring out the flavor of the fresh ingre-

dients in every dish she cooked, follow strict care instructions
for every kind of fabric so that his clothes and linens were
always in the best condition, and wash and iron the sheets
every three days. Her husband nagged at her incessantly that
the house, clothes, bedding would all be hers one day and
that she had to treasure them, be frugal, and maintain a perfect home. To Yonhwa, that "one day" when all of it would
be hers seemed so far into the future. She honestly felt the
day would never come. He was healthier and livelier than she
was. He spent his days picking on every little thing she was
doing wrong around the house, and his nights harassing her
with his insatiable sexual appetite. She found him disgusting,
but put up with it. She refused to go back to her dirty, cold,
unpredictable former life. But before long, her husband grew
visibly bored with her.

One evening, the couple was sitting on the living room
sofa drinking tea. A vapor trail stretched across the sky beyond
the window. When Yonhwa was young, her little brothers
argued over whether the white line across the sky was a cloud
or made by an airplane, and came to Yonhwa in the end to
settle the argument. Yonhwa didn't know, either, but said it
was a cloud, and the youngest made fun of his older brother
for being dumb. When the latter found out eventually that he
was right, he would not let Yonhwa hear the end of it. Yonhwa shared this story with her husband. Her siblings would
have left the facility a long time ago. They were probably out
there doing dangerous work and living with uncertainty like
she used to, she added.

He sat up and gazed into her eyes.

"So that's what you're after?" he said.

Yonhwa didn't answer.

He repeated his question two more times. She didn't answer, and he hit her for the first time. Yonhwa went into the kitchen and pulled out a small checkered napkin that served as a spoon coaster and folded it into a crane. The napkin was thick and firm enough that if she handled it carefully, she could manipulate it into shapes.

Some days, she folded one crane. Other days, she folded three or four. She lined them up on the windowsill, and on the day she folded the hundredth crane, she ran away from her husband.

Saha Estates was the only option once again. Unit 214 was still unoccupied, but she hid in the custodian's quarters. She hid herself utterly and completely. The residents asked if the rumors were true that Yonhwa was back, why Unit 214 was still empty, if anyone had seen her, etc. Three seasons went by without anyone able to confirm these rumors, and when Yonhwa's husband or the people he sent stopped looking for her, Yonhwa returned to Unit 214. She was pregnant. Yonhwa said it was her ex-husband's and that she would raise the child on her own at the Saha Estates. And so Sara was born. No one went to the trouble of counting the months backward, guessing who the father might be, or even spreading rumors.

THE YARD WAS a mess.

"I can't take another day of this. Fuck!"

The young cops swore loud enough for everyone to hear as they ripped the lettuce, cucumbers, and tomatoes from

Granny Konnim's garden, threw them on the ground, and stomped on them. They took their shirts off and splashed water on themselves at the faucets and sprayed each other by stoppering the faucets with their thumbs. They guffawed when they got one of the residents wet, and kicked the water containers when someone scowled at them or told them off.

Sara brought out food for the neighborhood cats on the way to work as she always did. She checked the empty dishes and filled them with kibble and water. She had to stick around and wait for the cats to show because she was concerned about the strangers poking around. Besides, the days were getting longer and the cats were more at risk of being spotted and captured. She stood under the awning of the custodian's office and waited.

Yabun, the cat who kept the best track of when Sara filled the dishes, poked his head out from behind Building A. He must have been pretty famished, being the kind of cat who never went through trash or ate thrown-out food, but he was in no rush. Limping over on his three legs but keeping his tail and back in a graceful line, he passed the trash cans, the row of bicycles that belonged to the residents, and the chair by the office door.

Yabun stuck his nose in the dish, sniffed, opened his mouth wide as if to yawn, then surveyed the area. His eyes met Sara's. She slowly closed and opened her eye to say hello to Yabun, who stood stiffly. The cat meowed like a baby and started eating his food. Just then, something flew at Yabun and hit him in his only front leg. Yabun yowled and jumped up. He dashed in the direction of Building B.

"Damn vermin!"

Two of the cops ran after Yabun, throwing rocks at him. Sara bolted at them and grabbed one by the arm.

"Stop it!"

Startled in place, the cop slowly turned toward Sara. He removed her hand from his arm and reached for her eye patch. Sara swatted it away.

The cop smirked. "Hey, one-eye. That gimpy cat yours?"

Sara tried to turn around without answering, but the cop grabbed *her* by the arm. His long, dirty fingernails dug into Sara's white flesh.

"Didn't you hear me? I said, is that cripple cat yours?"

They had a new target. The other cop dropped the rocks he was rolling around in his palm and blocked Sara's way. Sara tried to get past them, but didn't have the strength to get around two strong, intimidating young men.

One cop covered his right eye with his right hand and said, "You're the one-eyed bartender who works at the bar down the back street, right? You're real famous, you know that? I hear you only show people your bum eye in bed. Let me see that mysterious eye of yours."

The other cop went around her back, seized her by the shoulders with one arm, and held her chin in place with his free hand. Sara shouted and kicked, but she couldn't free herself. The first cop stepped up in front of her with his face inches before hers; Sara pretended to collapse forward and bit him. He clapped his hand on his shoulder and screamed.

"Stop it!" the old man screamed even louder than the cop as he came running with a big, tattered sack and a rusty pair of tongs from the basement of Building A.

"Stop it right now!" the old man shouted again as he slipped and fell. "I'm gonna call for help!"

The residents who had been watching through their windows, unwilling to step up, finally emerged into the yard. "That's enough! This is police brutality! You have no right to treat us this way!" The residents circled the scene, and the old man pulled Sara away by the wrist with his bloody, dirt-covered hands. Her makeup ruined with tears, she secured her eye patch in place and looked around at the people in the yard. Jin-kyung wasn't among them. Between disappointment and relief, Sara didn't know what to feel.

AT WORK LATER that evening, Sara couldn't focus. A wine-glass with a long stem seemed to turn into liquid as she took it down from the rack, and it slipped through her fingers. Looking down at the shattered glass, Sara felt the terror of the day like the aftershock of an earthquake.

She told her boss she wasn't feeling well and went home early. It wasn't even midnight yet, but the floodlight at the gate was off and the old man wasn't at his post. The cops, who were everywhere during the day, were nowhere to be seen, either. Like a stage before a show, the grounds were too dark and silent. A sense of disquiet came over Sara. She crept quietly across the yard on tiptoe. Suddenly someone came up behind her and covered her mouth. She felt hot breath on her ear and a cold blade against her throat.

"I'll see that bum eye of yours one way or another, bitch," said a familiar voice.

Sara walked in the direction she was shoved. A pair of feet following them, walked offbeat to their steps. There were two people behind her. Each time Sara struggled, the blade dug into her throat in minuscule increments. They moved quickly, as if they had a specific place in mind. Sara knew where they were taking her. Unit 101 was always open and usually empty. The cops' quarters.

Sara was dragged down the first-floor walkway. The man following moved ahead of them and, as Sara expected, slowly turned the doorknob at Unit 101. The rusty door opened with a creak. Inside, it was completely dark. Like a living thing, the darkness opened its mouth wide enough to swallow Sara. It was as if someone were strangling her. She wasn't scared to death as a figure of speech—she literally felt the terror of death. She dug her heels into the floor, and the man drew the blade against her neck ever so slightly. The sharp knife finally broke skin and Sara jerked as if electrocuted.

Inside the apartment, Sara was pushed to the floor and the front door was shut behind her with a loud slam.

"Oh no, blood," the assailant said quietly, wiping the blade on his pants leg. "Gee, I wonder where it came from?"

He was coming toward Sara again, the blade poised in front of him, when the front door whipped open and light flooded into the apartment. It appeared to be a flashlight, blindingly bright. Sara didn't care who was holding that flashlight. While the men scrambled, she shut her eye tight and ran for the door.

"Who's that? Turn that off!" And with the man's cry, the light went out. A huge shadow jumped up, rather nimbly for its size, and flew at the man. *Whack!* A dull thud was followed by the sound of metal clanking. The shadow twisted the man's wrist and he dropped the knife. The other man paused for a moment and threw himself in the direction of the knife. The shadow, still holding on to the wrist of the first man, kicked the second man in the hand, and then the gut. The shadow seized both men by their throats, simultaneously, and slammed them up against a wall, hitting the light switch on. The men's faces were red and their pupils were dilating like drowned bodies surfacing.

"STOP!" Sara yelled.

It was Woomi. She looked each man in the eye and said, enunciating every word, "Do you know why they can't demolish the Saha Estates? It's because of the monster that lives here. I. Am. The monster. You wanna see a real monster in action, you pull this sort of thing again."

Woomi threw the men across the room. Jin-kyung heard the screams and came running as the men lay on the floor gasping and coughing. Sara was shaking, with her hands wrapped around her neck, and Woomi was plopped down on the floor, fists clenched. Jin-kyung took in the sight and went to Woomi first to help her up.

"Are you okay?" she asked.

Woomi nodded once without making eye contact with Jin-kyung. Sara burst into tears. The old Sara would have said she was lucky. That it could have been much worse, that she was really, truly okay, that she was grateful for Jin-kyung's concern. She was born with one eye, she lost her mother at age twelve, and started working at a bar at seventeen. She took this wearying life in stride surprisingly well. No resentments, no regrets, sometimes even grateful for her lot.

Born and raised in the Saha Estates, Sara lived in a world that fell within the scope of the Estates—its shade, texture, level of challenge. But lately Sara had been starting to see the world beyond the Saha Estates grounds. Many things she had taken for granted were beginning to make her feel angry and wronged. Sara lifted her left hand to wipe away a tear from her left eye.

"Are you okay?" Woomi asked.

"I want a proper life," Sara said. "Not to be merely alive like a worm, or a moth, or a cactus, but to really live. I'm sorry, but I'm not okay today."

Sara's words stung Woomi in the heart. Her chest ached and she could hardly breathe. Woomi quickly turned away from Sara and Jin-kyung, waddled off, and disappeared into Granny Konnim's apartment. Jin-kyung went up to Sara, who was biting her bottom lip and trembling. She had a message for Do-kyung. *Hang in there just a little longer. I'm looking for another place for you to hide, so wait just a little longer,* she wanted Sara to tell him. Sending a note was risky, and the thought of calling Sara or visiting her made her nervous, so Jin-kyung had been waiting all day for them to run into each other. And here they were. Besides, Jin-kyung had rushed to Woomi first after the attack. Jin-kyung squeezed Sara's shoulders, unable to bring herself to ask for the favor.

Breath rushing out, perhaps a sigh or a sob, Sara said, "I know you have something to say to me. I know. But now's not the time."

Chagrined by her own selfishness, and ashamed that Sara saw right through her, Jin-kyung withdrew her hands.

THE NIGHT'S DISTURBANCE had passed, and Sara managed to calm herself and go to bed at two in the morning. In the heart of the summer when each new day logged record-breaking high temperatures, Sara, strangely, wasn't hot at all. She pulled the covers up to her chin as an almost imperceptible tremor that originated from deep within her heart spread out over her body. She thought of Jin-kyung passing her by and going to Woomi's aid. The memory broke apart and sank bit by bit like an iceberg melting and crumbling, and in Sara's mind Jin-kyung's face went from shock to uncertainty, then concern, tenderness. There was something special in the way she looked at Woomi. *What did Jin-kyung feel for Woomi? Where did it come from? And why not me?*

Sara got out of bed and sat in front of the mirror. The eye patch covered her right eye. Sara only took off her eye patch to wash up, and since there was no mirror in the bathroom, she rarely had to see her face without the patch. She brought her hand up to the fabric. *Can I stand to look at it? Can I accept it?* It was like looking back in a scary alley, prying open a forbidding door, peeling off a scab. She knew better, but simply had to see for herself.

Sara unhooked the elastic over her right ear. The eye patch fell away down her cheek. Flesh. Just milky-white flesh. No feature to distinguish from forehead or cheek. Clean, smooth. Sara found an eyebrow pencil in her makeup kit and placed the tip where there should have been an eye. She drew a right pupil and lines around it symmetrical to the left side with her nose ridge as the axis. A large eye, several eyelid folds, eyelashes that were long but few in number, a vivid pupil. Sara blinked, but her new eye did not. One blue eye glistening and welling up, another eye a frighteningly dark gray that would never, ever close. As one unfocused eye fixed its dead stare at the void, the other eye shut tight, tears streaming.

Blood had leaked through the bandage on her neck. She ripped it off as if in protest, tugging at the skin underneath and opening the gash that was just barely held together. Blood sprang from the wound and dripped onto her shirt.

"It isn't my fault," Sara suddenly blurted, sobbing. She rubbed her right eye hard with the back of her hand. She stopped crying when half her face was covered with the smudge, like a great bruise, and only then did she realize Do-kyung was gone. She ran to the door and turned the door-knob, then stopped. *I can't tell anyone. I can't ask for help.* Sara helplessly collapsed among the shoes by the door.

SARA DRIFTED OFF to sleep when light started trickling in through her curtains. She woke up with a headache, and went out to the veranda for some air. She opened the window all the way but couldn't feel the breeze. She opened the screen as well, believing the gentle wind caressing her face would wake her up, but the wind was blowing in the wrong direction. She leaned out a little, and fell, with the broken railing, off the veranda onto the first floor. Actually, Sara couldn't remember what had just happened. She probably leaned against the rail-ing without a thought in her head. Luckily, she stepped away with no more than bruises on her chin and elbows. But there was an irritating, throbbing pain coming from somewhere inside her that she couldn't pinpoint.

Sara slowly made her way up the stairwell and knocked on Jin-kyung's door on the seventh floor. There was no answer until Sara said, "Jin-kyung."

The door opened. Startled by Sara's purple, swollen chin, Jin-kyung opened her mouth, but Sara spoke first.

"Do-kyung disappeared last night."

Did he leave on his own? Did someone break in and take him? When did you first realize that he was gone? What was the condition of the apartment then? Jin-kyung wanted to know but couldn't ask.

"Are you okay? Your face . . . was it because of Do-kyung?"

Sara lowered her gaze and rubbed her chin, shaking her head. "No, this doesn't have anything to do with him."

Jin-kyung, not knowing what to do with herself, rubbed the wall with her fingertip as Sara simply stared.

"I'm sorry."

"No, I'm sorry. I'm sorry I—"

Tears fell from Sara's eye. Jin-kyung stretched out her hand, and Sara backed away reflexively, protecting her eye patch. Jin-kyung held her palms open and mumbled, "I wasn't trying to," while Sara touched her eye patch, wiped her tear, picked at her cuticles, and generally didn't know what to do with herself.

"Why are we sorry?" Sara asked. "We haven't done anything wrong to each other, so why are we sorry? Who's the one who really needs to apologize to me? No one apologizes to me. I don't know who owes me an apology anymore. So I . . . I keep tearing up out of anger."

Jin-kyung had done something wrong. She was sorry, and

still wanted to apologize, but held her tongue lest she make Sara cry again.

WAN, UNIT 201. THIRTY YEARS EARLIER.

People stood hand in hand, fingers laced. The night was pitch-black and they couldn't make out the person standing right in front of them. The moon was out, obscured by clouds, and one could see the occasional star, not quite bright enough to cast any light on the ocean. The dim light at the port, like a hushed voice, made the dark water seem murky. Unsure of where to go, the light lay just below the surface of the water instead of casting bright glitter on the waves. Families, lovers, and friends holding tight to each other so as not to be separated rushed toward the light all at once like swarms of hatchlings. Careful footsteps on pavement, shoulders of strangers brushing against each other, panicked breathing, sniffles that could no longer be held in. The ocean was mostly quiet, and even the babies did not cry.

Every Monday before dawn a small cargo ship set sail for the mainland with more Town people than cargo. The passengers were those who received a deportation notice, or were about to, or feared they could be deported any day. That ship alone did not require an entry process. Passengers casually exited the boat at the mainland harbor like getting off the train at one's hometown. If there was an agreement between Town and the mainland, few knew about it. But the small cargo ship brought those who didn't qualify as Town

Citizens to the mainland harbor every Monday morning, no questions asked.

When the boat finally set off, and a good distance had opened between the ship and the dock, the passengers settled down on the deck to rest their weary bodies and hearts for a moment. Leaning against enormous containers carrying who knew what, some smoked, others cried, and women breastfed their infants.

All they could see from the deck was the dark sea. Looking out into the night, the recklessly crammed passengers could not believe they were on water. Calm and smooth, the sea looked like a big mass of jelly, as if, were someone to drop something off the side, it would bounce off the surface and soar right back up. But below this tranquil surface living things holding secrets billions of years old swam in the deep trenches, huge carnivorous plants without intelligence opened their mouths to trap food, whirlpools sucked things down, volcanoes erupted, mountains rose, and the ground split. Depths the average mortal soul could not fathom. An ocean floor that toes would never, ever reach no matter how far they sank.

The passengers began to nod off. It was beginning to turn light, but the sun hadn't risen above the horizon. Then the ship vanished.

A long time passed before news of the vanished ship reached Town. Most passengers had snuck onto the ship, so they did not have family waiting for them at the harbor. There was no departure record, either. The sea was calm and the sun was rising. There were no strong currents or frequent pirate sightings in the area, and the journey was a mere three- or four-hour distance. But somehow, the ship had vanished without a trace.

The mainland news suspected the ship had gone missing, but that was all. There was no evidence—no passenger, container, debris, life vest, lifeboat, or any belonging that a passenger or crew member would have been carrying. The fact that there was a ship that set sail for the mainland every Monday before dawn, that even the light at the dock was kept dim, and that people joined their cold hands as they boarded the ship grew faint. Those who were suspicious began to question their own minds as time passed, telling themselves they were mistaken or dreaming. The desperate hopes of recovery scattered in the wind like hearsay.

When every last trace of the ship had vanished completely, mysterious flyers appeared in Town. White paper boats glued to black construction paper. And one sentence: *Where did the ship go?*

On the first day, hundreds of flyers were tacked to the trees lining the road to the Parliament; a strip of flyers taped together was wrapped around the broadcasting station fence on the second day, and a busy downtown street was paved with the flyers on the third. Courthouse, prison, university, port—a great mass of flyers appeared at a new spot every day. They went up as if in guerrilla action in the night, and public offices took them down as their first task in the morning. Word spread that a ship had disappeared. Missing persons reports were filed in droves. The police stations, public offices, and the provisional embassy of the mainland were overrun with family, friends, and colleagues of missing persons who demanded to know their whereabouts, but they couldn't find answers anywhere.

The flyers continued to emerge even after stricter penalties were implemented. They kept coming, and nothing was revealed about the persons behind them—whether it was one person, if it was multiple individuals, or an organized group.

Word spread that Town government had placed a ban on folding paper boats. A kindergarten teacher and a principal were supposedly fined for having students fold boats with colored paper and pinning them up on a board decorated like the ocean. The teacher had to explain the purpose of the lesson to the authorities. The police interrogation was grueling; the affronted teacher attempted suicide and was committed to a general hospital. Rumors circulated as to which hospital. None of it was true. There was no ban on making paper boats, but the remarkable part was this: people had no trouble believing that there were paper boat bans and kindergarten teachers paying fines.

On the day the Council of Ministers released a statement that the ban on paper boats was unfounded and that those responsible for circulating such rumors would be punished to the full extent of the law, the person behind the very first paper boat flyer was discovered. She was an average housewife with a six-year-old daughter. Her husband was part of the administrative staff at the university, and she had a younger brother who attended the same university. Six years younger than her, the brother had been living under her care since their parents retired two years earlier to a warm country a six-hour flight away.

The brother hadn't taken the transformation of his hometown well. She gently assured him not to worry too much. After all, the same people would be living as they always had in the same place. How bad could it get?

"I'm not saying things will get bad," the brother had said, hanging his head in despair. "Or that someone is going to harm me. I'm just not the kind of person who can live here. You can't live underwater if you don't have gills. Doesn't matter how clean or warm or safe. It's not possible."

And on that day, he got on that ship.

When asked if she was the first to post the flyers, she said she didn't know.

"How do you not know what you've done?"

"I did fold a paper boat and put it up. But I don't know if I was the first. I taped one in front of the Parliament because I was at my wits' end and out of options. That's all."

The investigator produced a paper boat that was worn down at the creases and falling apart, and slid it across the table in front of her.

"Did you fold this?"

"I don't know."

"Why don't you know what you have or have not folded?"

"Everyone folds paper boats the same way. Grab any random person off the street, and tell them to fold a paper boat. They'll fold it like this."

Her hands were chapped raw, shoulders slanted, lips a tense line. The investigator's head suddenly went reeling. *How can she be so unrepentant and fine? Does she really not know where she is right now, what's happening to her, and where she will end up?*

"Where did the ship go?" she asked. "The people on the ship? My brother? Why is no one speaking up about this?"

"Get a grip, lady. You want to vanish, too?"

She was arrested immediately, and after a single trial was executed two months later.

IT WAS A time of confusion and fear. Many non-government organizations sedulously released statements expressing concern and outrage regarding the events that were unfolding in Town, and for that their very existence came under threat. The head of the oldest, most trusted Citizens' coalition was assassinated around that time, and the incident was briefly investigated and closed as a result of power struggles within the coalition. No one believed the investigation report to be true, but no one dared speak up. Then everything that had been held back and repressed came bursting out when an ordinary mother was executed.

The enraged took to the streets. The hollowed-out bodies wandered through Town. Desperation, guilt, fury of similar kinds and proportions. When these emotions gathered and pooled, a dynamic as natural as gravity or magnetism formed. Hearts moved limbs, which in turn moved other hearts. Even those who had not lost their family took to the streets. This later came to be known as the Butterfly Riot.

L2s, Sahas, and even Citizens came out and filled the eight-lane street leading to the Parliament. *Council of Ministers, show your faces. Equal citizenship for equal people. Down with Special Law!* People stood in rows of one hundred. The first row rammed into the Parliament wall together at the signal, then came the row after that, then another and another. The row at the very front hit the wall and dispersed, then went to the back of the queue and stood in formation again. All night, people rammed against the wall. Shoulders were bruised, the trees and surrounding buildings shook, but the wall enclosing the Parliament did not come down.

Morning brought despair, exhaustion, and actual pain that spread a sense of enervation among the protesters. The size of their crowd had shrunk noticeably, and there was no heart in the slogans they shouted. The rows charging at the walls had grown much slower. An old blue truck pulled up by the protesters, unloaded something, and left. Seven masked effigies, pictures of the head of the corporation and the spokesperson for the Council of Ministers, and a model of the Parliament building. Excitement instantly spread among the protesters. They lifted the effigies and pictures above their heads and passed them quickly to the center, threw them on the ground in a pile, and began to flick their lighters.

Dark smoke billowed and hung about like gossip, then the stack sent flames shooting up overhead, engulfing the effigies in an undulating haze. The paper from the model of the Parliament—or maybe the straw that stuffed the effigies—turned to ash that fluttered up into the air. Like little butterflies.

A flock of helitankers flew down from the northern sky in formation. They circled lazily along the walls of the Parliament and dropped a torrent of water on the protesters' heads. To put out a small bonfire. The ash butterflies fell heavy to the ground and drowned in puddles of dark water. The cops attacked with batons. Too many protesters were injured and killed. A young man groping the ground for his eye, which had popped out when a baton hit him on the back of the head, was trampled to death.

The protesters scattered, schools and hospitals and crosses were knocked down, and the most ordinary of lives were destroyed. On this rubble, Town formed its strong, pervasive roots.

The Butterfly Riot came to serve as a metaphor for extreme chaos, anxiety, and fear. No one knew where the term *butterfly* came from. Some said it was from the ashes, others said it came from the butterfly effect the protest had on Town and other countries beyond it.

There are no official records on what happened to the husband of the woman who inspired the Butterfly Riot. Word spread that he killed his daughter and took his own life, while some insisted he was also punished under Special Law, but neither rumor was confirmed.

ON THE DAY of the woman's execution, the young investigator who interrogated her was hit by a cab on his way back to the office after a meeting. The driver stated that the investigator jumped in front of him. He looked like he was going to hail a cab from the way he had one foot hanging off the curb, but he was simply staring at the car without raising his hand, so the driver wasn't sure. That was the reason he switched to the outermost lane but did not slow down. The investigator, who wasn't fatally injured, also stated that it was his fault, and the cabdriver was not penalized. The investigator's leg was mangled and left him with a permanent limp, as it wasn't treated properly.

SHORTLY AFTER THE Butterfly Riot, a man who couldn't speak and a girl who rarely spoke came to the Saha Estates. With a gentle look on his face, the man knocked on the custodian's office door, bowed, and held up a note that said, *We would like to live here. Please.* The piece of paper was too big compared to the brevity of the message, and it seemed the man had run out of ink, as the strokes of his letters were written over several times. But his handwriting was so neat anyone would have believed he was a calligrapher; it was straight and evenly spaced as if printed. The girl, who was about six or seven, referred to him as Daddydaddy. Not just Daddy, but Daddydaddy.

A meeting was held to decide whether to take the father and daughter in, but the residents couldn't come to an agreement. The young, taciturn girl and the adult who couldn't speak weren't able to fully explain who they were and how they ended up at the Saha Estates. The eldest resident of Saha and the residents' representative, Queen Grandma, sat them down.

"Is she your only family?" she asked the father in a kind voice.

The man wrote his answer neatly but far too slowly on a piece of paper. *Please let me and my daughter live here. Please.*

"Right," she said. "So it's just the two of you? Your family is just her?"

The man wrote slowly once again, *Yes, thank you.*

They went back-and-forth a few more times without getting anywhere. Queen Grandma sighed and turned to the girl.

"Do you live with just your daddy?"

"Yes, me and my Daddydaddy. The two of us live together."

"Where's your mommy?"

The child clammed up. *Do you have any other family?
Where did you live before? What did your daddy do?* The child
didn't answer any of these questions. Instead, she told them in
clear pronunciation her favorite food, her favorite color, her
favorite song, which she sang, clapping to the beat, and then
thanked the adults who praised her. But when someone asked
what her name was, she clammed up again. She would not
answer any questions regarding her identity. She only smiled,
and her father looked at her with pride. In her entire life,
Queen Grandma had never met a person who couldn't speak.
She was astonished by the realization that she'd reached the
age she was without ever having met a person who couldn't
speak, or couldn't hear, or couldn't see.

The residents spoke with the father and daughter for a
long time using gestures, facial expressions, and writing. They
were able to ascertain two things for sure: that they had a history they couldn't share with anyone even if they could speak,
and that they had no place to go besides Saha Estates. And
then there were the things they could guess at: they were nice
people, down on their luck, and wouldn't cause trouble as
neighbors. The father and daughter received the key to Unit
205.

THE FATHER ALWAYS carried the daughter in his arms. She
wasn't a toddler, but still her father carried her everywhere,
her already long legs swinging. The grown-ups chided, *Why
are you carrying such a big child? You should walk on your
own, kid.* The father and daughter only smiled sweetly at their
neighbors and carried on as they always had.

They often played on the seesaw in the little playground. The daughter sat on one side and the father pressed down the other side gently. Pressed and let go, pressed and let go. When she got used to it, he pressed and released faster. *Bop, bop, bop, bop.* The girl smiled so wide her teeth showed. Then he stomped with his foot. The small girl bounced up and down in a mad rodeo. She laughed so hard she could hardly breathe, and the father smiled with his mouth wide open.

"Having fun, huh?" the custodian remarked, perhaps to mock or to encourage, as he passed them by. The pair beamed without a word.

They were often sighted drawing on the grounds. The girl had a fifty-piece color pencil set for professionals—unlike anything anyone in Saha owned—and the father followed her around and helped, carrying the colored pencils, construction paper, a panel of wood to fix the paper to, an art pencil with a soft, dark lead, and an eraser. The girl sat down anywhere—by the playground, in front of the stone pillar, at their door, in a corner in the yard—and the father arranged the art supplies around her so she could work. The girl examined the scenery carefully, squinting and measuring proportions with her pencil. She looked like quite the artist, and produced drawings more or less at the level of her age group.

Once he settled into life at Saha Estates, the father went to work like the others. His post was at a warehouse his neighbor introduced him to. When goods from various corporations arrived in containers, he sorted and delivered them to other warehouses. The goods were then taken out of the containers, sorted and loaded onto trucks, and unloaded at other warehouses. Due to the limited size of the trucks and warehouses, the workers had to be smart about stacking wares, like fitting puzzle pieces while moving very quickly. As the body moved, the eyes had to survey the space for empty spots and gauge width and height for the right place. By the end of the day, both muscles and brain were exhausted.

When Saha parents were at work, the children were looked after by Queen Grandma in Unit 201, and other residents sometimes pitched in. Queen Grandma volunteered herself, claiming she was getting paid as the residents' representative and doing no work in return. But it was impossible for someone her age to watch several children. Whoever didn't have work that day took turns at mealtimes. People who could draw taught them to draw, people with good handwriting taught them to write, and people who were good with numbers taught them math. The children varied in age and cognitive abilities, but got along well and looked out for each other.

The girl from Unit 205 didn't require a lot of care. She spent most of her time by herself, drawing. When the younger kids ruined her pictures or broke her colored pencils, she didn't get angry at them. She played within the boundaries the grown-ups set, didn't have requests, and ate what she was fed. Her father could go to work knowing she was in good hands, and the child spent uneventful days with other kids. But then an accident occurred. There were an unusual number of trucks at the warehouse one day, and parking was tight. The father went in back of one truck to help an inexperienced driver reverse into a spot by banging on the side of the truck as a signal, but the driver was so tense he didn't hear it. *Bang, bang. Bangbangbangbangbangbang.* Then the banging stopped.

The girl was only seven. She couldn't live by herself. The only place she could possibly go in the Saha Estates was Unit 201. Queen Grandma was the only person with the time and space for a kid. She was at a loss.

"We'll raise her together," the mother of twins in Unit 304 persuaded Queen Grandma. "We'll play with her, feed her, bathe her, and teach her to read and write. But she needs to sleep in the same place every night. And at least one person she can think of as her family."

Queen Grandma lifted her eyes and counted, staring into space. *Eight, nine, ten, eleven, twelve, thirteen, fourteen,* she said to herself. Would seven years be enough?

"I'm not worried about her being a burden. It's just that I will most certainly die first. How could a child like that bear to see yet another person she lived with die?"

No one had thought of that. The residents sat in silence as Queen Grandma slowly nodded to show she'd made up her mind. The child gathered her things and came to Unit 201. She played with the kids in 304 while Queen Grandma made space for her. She ate dinner with them, and then came back to 201.

"From now on, this is your home, I'm your grandma, and you and I will sleep in this room together, okay?"

"Okay, thank you."

Queen Grandma was relieved that the girl did not say something like, *I don't want to live with an old lady I hardly know,* or burst into tears looking for her daddy. But she wished the girl had not said, "Thank you." Queen Grandma's heart broke at how well-behaved the child was. When the residents chipped in and brought her new clothes and blankets, she picked up a green vest among them, buried her face in it, and looked delighted. *She's still a child, all right*, Queen Grandma thought, somewhat relieved.

Queen Grandma couldn't fall asleep that night, worried as she was that the child might be uncomfortable in the new bedding in a new place, or that perhaps she smelled bad to the child. She carefully rolled over, minding the rustling of the covers, and saw the girl sound asleep with her mouth hanging open. Only then did she relax and let sleep come over her. In her dream, she was holding a child or puppy that kept slipping and threatening to fall to the ground, and the moment she realized she was dreaming, her eyes flew open. She heard sobbing. The child had her back turned to the old lady, shoulders trembling. When Queen Grandma propped herself up and looked over the child's shoulder, she saw her crying with both hands over her mouth to muffle the sound. A child so young, crying so bitterly. The old lady wrapped the girl in her arms and wept with her. The child seemed to be falling asleep in the old lady's arms. Then she opened her eyes, lifted her hand, and stroked the old lady's face.

"My name is Wan," she said.

"That's a pretty name."

"Thank you. Daddy told me not to tell anyone, that bad things will happen if I told, but I'll tell you because now nobody knows my name. Grandma, my name is Wan. Call me Wan sometimes when we are alone."

"Okay, Wan. Go to sleep now, Wan."

"Thank you."

She could see the child's eyes moving about under her closed eyelids. She hoped the girl would stop saying thank you.

QUEEN GRANDMA PASSED away seven years later, survived by Wan. She had done her best to live as long as she could. One night, she fell asleep next to Wan and did not wake up in the morning. She looked as peaceful as if she were sleeping, but Wan saw right away that she had passed. She didn't panic, just went down to the first floor to let the custodian know. Young Wan ended up mourning another death, as Queen Grandma had feared. But the girl took it better than expected. She comforted the grown-ups, who were so sorry for her they didn't know what to do, and said she could and would like to live alone in the apartment she had shared with Grandma. Unit 201, Grandma and Wan's place, became just Wan's place.

She wasn't lonely or scared. Things Queen Grandma had tucked away in odd corners of the house would turn up from time to time and cheer her. Deep in the bathroom closet, she found rolls of toilet paper Grandma had stolen each time she went to a public bathroom. A glass bottle filled with buttons was found in the kitchen cupboard. A stack of take-out menus. They made Wan laugh. Grandma had not once ordered take-out. Looking through the expenses book recorded with Grandma's crooked hand and bad spelling, Wan laughed the loudest at, *Damn Expensive Winter Jacket for Little Wan*. When she found a pair of chopsticks and a spoon, a handkerchief, and a tube of lipstick, a part of her wished that Grandma had lived

to continue using them. She wished she could go on finding little traces of Grandma for another year, or even just a month.

Wan became a grown-up in Unit 201.

IA, UNIT 201

Ia vanished at the end of the summer.

It was the time of year when the veranda windows that
were left open all day long were closed at night. The days were
still hot, but the early morning cooled the air so that the light
blankets that people kicked to the foot of their beds in the
night were drawn back up to their shoulders.

Ia wore a thick winter jacket through the spring, and
when summer came he wore the same T-shirt every day with
the hems unstitched, paired with his mother's old jeans shorts
that came down below his knees. The flip-flops he wore all
throughout the year were worn thin. The messy hair that
came down to his shoulders, Ia cut himself.

Just after Ia's first birthday, when his hair had grown past
his eyes, Ia's mother took him to the hairdresser in Building
A for his first trim. Sitting up very straight in the chair with
his double chin, thick neck, and stiff shoulders, Ia looked so
cute the hairdresser gave his cheek a gentle pinch. His pupils
dilated in shock as if he'd suddenly stepped into darkness. His
eyes were fixed not on his mother or the hairdresser, but on
something far outside the window. Though he had learned to
speak quite early, he did not cry out for his mother.

Water drops as fine as dust sprayed from the bottle and

landed on Ia's delicate hair. One light brush with the comb. The glittering silver scissors held in the hairdresser's long white fingers touched Ia's forehead. Ia made a sharp earsplitting sound that one wouldn't believe a human being could make. The sustained shriek carried like a broken car alarm on a lazy afternoon. "Gone berserk" did not begin to describe Ia's reaction. From that day on, Ia made the same sound every time he saw the hairdresser or his mother with a pair of scissors. At seven, Ia started cutting his own hair, always very badly.

Ia was ten now, but did not look it; he was tall and had his mother's long legs. In outfits that did not reflect the seasons and with bangs hiding his eyes, Ia tottered around precariously on tiptoe. He never cried out when startled, never answered when someone called, didn't respond to questions even if he knew the answer, but he did randomly interrupt other people's conversations to correct their wrong usage of expressions or scramble the words they just said to form a new sentence. When the other children learned to read and do math in the Saha Estates study room, Ia sat in the corner by himself absorbed in a book or doodle, then left without a word. Ia's mother asked the teachers to just ignore him.

The residents of the Saha Estates felt bad for the boy, who hung around like a sticky festering puddle, but pretended not to see him. If Ia suddenly sat down in the street, if he ate something he picked up off the ground, if he suddenly walked into someone's unlocked apartment, if he jumped out of an alley late at night, they pretended nothing happened. It was the polite thing to do. Ia wandered both on and off the Saha Estates grounds as he pleased; his mother slept through the day like a log, with the blackout curtains drawn, and dragged her weary self from one parlor to the next all night. The dinner she prepared for him went cold, then dried up. Politeness turned to indifference.

THE PINK PEARL lipstick that she must have applied had smudged up to the tip of her nose, and the boldly curved eyebrows struck a sharp contrast with her oily face. In heels at least ten centimeters high, Ia's mother ran about like a madwoman. *Clickclickclickclickclickclick*. Her footsteps sounded like urgent knocking, sending the quiet Estates into a frenzy.

Back home late from work and still in their uniforms, half-drunk, or half-asleep, the residents helped look for Ia. The custodian, who was calling Ia's name much louder than the others, was beginning to lose his voice.

After a long day of being exposed to the harsh afternoon light on a window-cleaning and painting job, Jin-kyung was so tired she couldn't fall asleep. She felt as if the chemicals in the paint were still in her lungs and veins, carrying poison throughout her body each time she took a breath. When she went out into the walkway for some air in the middle of the night, she saw the commotion.

The rectangular courtyard looked like a TV screen. People in the yard as seen from the seven floors above looked ridiculous, like very short people with disproportionately large heads. It was like watching a silent film that featured actors busily wandering in and out of the shot. Woomi came up to the seventh floor, saw Jin-kyung at the end of the walkway, and said, "Ia, is that you?"

"It's me," Jin-kyung said and took a drag of her cigarette as if to prove it.

Woomi hung her head. "Have you seen a kid about a hundred and fifty centimeters tall, long hair, skinny? You've seen him around. The boy who's always wearing flip-flops even in the winter. Have you seen him?"

"Ia. I know him. I haven't seen him today."

Woomi conveyed her disappointment by heaving a sigh. As she ran back down the walkway in the other direction, she turned and asked, "How did you know his name?"

Like Woomi said, she ran into him from time to time. Two of their encounters Jin-kyung could never forget if she tried.

Jin-kyung left her front door unlocked most of the time in the summer. In fact, the door was almost never locked at Unit 701. Out of some unidentifiable anxiety, Jin-kyung had been vigilant about keeping the door locked when she first moved in, but lost her key twice. She had to borrow the emergency key from the custodian, get an earful from him, and have a copy made. Then she wondered if she really needed to keep her door locked when she and Do-kyung were the only ones living on the seventh floor and the closest occupied unit was on the sixth floor, an apartment that belonged to a young woman and a little girl. The custodian himself often skipped the seventh floor when he was making his rounds. Since then, Jin-kyung simply closed the door without locking it.

One day, napping with the veranda window and front door open to let in a breeze, Jin-kyung heard a familiar song playing in her dream. *Mea culpa. I kneel before my lord. Forgive us our sins. Deliver us from evil.* The hymn Mother used to sing. Mother sang it at Father's funeral. Do-kyung sang it at Mother's funeral.

Jin-kyung woke up from the dream as if she were fleeing from it. There was a stranger. Something was sitting on the veranda singing to Jin-kyung, something or someone, alive or dead, man or woman, old or young, Jin-kyung couldn't tell. Then everything went black. As if she were passing through a tunnel without lights, a gap opened up in Jin-kyung's consciousness. When she could see again, she was sitting on top of him with her hands strangling his scrawny neck. A grotesque face, dark red eyes open so wide they were about to pop, lips twitching laboriously, saying something. Although very distorted, the face belonged to a child who lived in Saha. Someone who was no threat to Jin-kyung. She jumped off him like a hopping insect.

Still lying on the veranda floor, the child moved his lips ceaselessly. His voice began to return.

"How do you know this song?" Jin-kyung asked.

The child did not answer but kept singing.

"Where did you hear it?"

The singing didn't stop. Jin-kyung took a deep breath, steadied herself, and waited. The child finally finished his song, sat up, tilted his head this way and that, and ran his hand over the nape of his neck. His uneven bangs were covering his right eye, but the child didn't brush them back.

"Who are you?" Jin-kyung asked.

"I'm Ia."

"How did you get in here?"

"The door was open. Wide."

As if to illustrate the point, a gust of wind blew in through the veranda and went out the front door. Sitting right in the middle of the wind's path, Jin-kyung felt a chill down her spine and only then realized that her shirt was soaking with sweat. Ia hummed the hymn as he headed for the front door. Suddenly cold from the sweat evaporating, or shaking in the grip of the rage and terror of her past, Jin-kyung shouted, trembling, "I said, how do you know that song!"

Ia stopped dead in his tracks and turned around to look at Jin-kyung. "You sing it all the time."

Ia casually let himself out. The sound of his flip-flops dragging echoed in the walkway, and tears fell from Jin-kyung's face. A root of memory that grew in the soil of an atrocious life was still lodged somewhere in Jin-kyung's nerves. She had run for her life and thought she'd escaped, only to look down and discover her own hand clutching to the hand of the very person she was running from. She was furious at Ia, even though he wasn't the one who placed the hand in Jin-kyung's.

The second encounter was on a rainy day. It had been muggy for days, the air suffused with the stench of rain, wet earth, and damp laundry. Jin-kyung came out to get away from the stifling apartment. She paced the yard holding up an umbrella that had caved in on one side. The old man called her into his office and offered her a cup of Darjeeling.

"I brewed it with expensive bottled water, so drink up."

Jin-kyung wrapped her hands around the cup and savored the aroma. An umbrella staggered past the Saha Estates stone pillar and went straight into Building A. Under the umbrella, still held open on the walkway, two sets of legs and arms intertwined. The umbrella kept catching on the railing, so the woman folded it, but it burst open again. The two people cackled. The woman closed it properly this time and swept the water off with her hand, and the man, who was watching this, snatched the umbrella from her and tossed it into the yard. They disappeared into an unoccupied unit on the first floor where the lock was broken, and a dark shadow came out from the other end of the walkway and stood in front of that very door. It was Ia.

Warm tea swirled and splashed onto Jin-kyung's hand as she put her cup down too quickly. A pleasant scent rose in the office. Jin-kyung wiped the back of her hand on her trousers leg and got up, but the old man grabbed her by the arm.

"He's still a child," she said. "Fifteen, tops? He shouldn't be over there—"

"Ten."

"So you know?"

"Leave him alone."

The woman was Ia's mother.

Ia sat leaning against the door where the two people had disappeared. He closed his eyes, tilted his head back, and tapped his foot in the air. As if he were listening to a bouncy tune.

The old man wiped the condensation on the inside of the office window. Minuscule droplets forced together clung to each other and left a fine trail as they fell like a tear. Ia on the other side of the window seemed as faint as a flashback in a movie. Scenes in life, unlike in movies, tended to play to ill-matched soundtracks. Jin-kyung felt a knot in the pit of her stomach as she heard what Ia must have been hearing.

THE EVENING AFTER Ia disappeared, his mother wore her makeup as meticulously as ever and went to work. All the makeup in the world couldn't mask the shadow on her face. The old man felt sorry for Ia's mother and spent days neglecting his duties to look for him. Precariously stacked bags of trash toppled over, exploded, and bits of trash were rolling around in the yard, but no one complained. Day, night, and dawn, Ia's mother and the old man called his name, their voices echoing throughout Saha.

Just over a month later, Ia's mother was seen coming home staggering drunk. Rumors spread and the residents started to blame her. Sure, the living had to go on living, but wasn't it too soon for the mother to go around roaring drunk? *Maybe she likes that sort of work. That poor dead boy Ia.* Instantly, Ia's mother became someone who liked to "drink" for a living, and Ia was assumed to be a dead kid. He did not come back. The grown-ups of the Saha Estates, including Ia's mother and the old man, gave up on Ia.

But then the hushed wild speculations about the mother and boy dispersed all at once. Ia's mother had begun to go to work in the morning and come back in the evening. A stroke of good luck had landed her a job at the City Hall information desk. She had worked the counter at a restaurant previously, which was actually a parlor of ill repute, so the restaurant-counter work was similar to her new job. Ia's mother said she'd been lucky. No one ever believed that she only worked the counter at the parlor, but it was even harder to believe that she got a job in City Hall by chance. A Saha, no matter how lucky, could not become a Citizen. A lucky Saha still would only ever be a Saha. And that job was not open to Sahas.

Her job wasn't the only thing that changed. The night Ia disappeared, his mother was wearing a pair of sparkly purple stockings, a stained silver silk dress, and a leopard-print scarf full of lint balls. And a pair of scuffed-up heels. She had always dressed like that—flashy but worn down, pretty but mismatched. But Ia's mother dressed completely different for her job at City Hall. A persimmon-colored skirt and jacket that was adequately form-fitting, a pale blue silk blouse, with sheer pantyhose. Black pumps with pointed toes bearing cute little ribbons. Simple but clean, boring but neat.

She often took a cab home. Cab fare was so expensive even Citizens rarely took them. But somehow Ia's mother was able to afford this luxury that most Citizens, not to mention Sahas, wouldn't dream of.

Jin-kyung found Ia's mother so strange, and stranger still the fact that no one was talking about it.

IA'S MOTHER WAS hardly able to push just two water containers. Woomi stood behind her, arms crossed. When her long, slender heel snapped to the right and Ia's mother flailed, Woomi strode up to her, snatched the cart from her hands, and marched up ahead with it. Jin-kyung watched them. Something in the way Ia's mother was biting her lip as she followed Woomi with her head bowed bothered Jin-kyung so much that she couldn't look away. Woomi arrived at Building A's Unit 201 first, left the cart there, and walked off down the walkway. Ia's mother belatedly said thank you to the back of Woomi's head.

After, Woomi approached Jin-kyung, who was filling her own water containers as if she hadn't noticed anything.

"What?" Woomi said.

"What?"

"You thought I was about to do something to Ia's mom?"

"Why?"

"Why indeed?"

Jin-kyung didn't answer.

"You were suspicious of me," Woomi said. "And you got nervous."

"No, I was just . . . it's weird. Ia disappeared and threw everyone into a panic just a few months ago, and he's still missing. But you and his mother and everyone else are so perfectly fine."

Jin-kyung had heard something odd from the custodian. *They were all going to hell in a handbasket. Saha Estates would be torn down because of the people who live here. Parents were selling children.* The old man stopped there, but Jin-kyung could tell he was referring to Ia's mother. When she asked him if he'd given up on finding Ia, he said that he wasn't going to waste any more time. Jin-kyung asked Woomi the same question, at which Woomi looked down, thought for a moment, and said, "That's not up to me, to decide if it's time to give up."

"The old man was talking like he knew something."

Woomi let out a chuckle that turned into a sigh. "I also thought for a moment that it was strange. What if it had been me—if I were her, if I came home late at night and my young son was missing, a boy like Ia? If my child, who wandered all over the place like he'd lost his mind and yet miraculously never failed to find his way home every night had gone missing, I would have dashed out barefoot. And yet that night she was wearing high platform sandals with ribbons wrapped perfectly around her ankles."

Jin-kyung played the scene from that night in her head. Mother walks in through the door with one strap of her dress slipping down her tired shoulder, her old scarf coming undone. She calls her son's name. The lights are out and the apartment is eerily cold. There's no sound. Mother rushes around the house opening doors to the bedroom, the bathroom, and the closet, but Ia isn't there. She runs over to the door calling Ia's name, and sees a pair of sneakers with the heels crushed and folded in, flip-flops upside down and thrown to opposite corners, and a shiny pair of platform sandals. Ia's mother fits her small feet into the sandals, patiently wraps the straps around her ankles to make bows.

"Hey, what are you thinking about?"

Woomi's voice brought Jin-kyung back to the present. She shook her head to mean, *Nothing.*

"Don't take it too seriously." Woomi stretched and smiled, flexing all the muscles on her face. "It's just a thought. No one knows. Same thing with Unit 316, right? No one knows why the woman died or if she died. Isn't it strange? There were so many rumors going around, but now no one dares bring it up. How did we end up so afraid of people with secrets?"

And that's why people are afraid of you, Jin-kyung thought as she looked at Woomi's great front teeth and dark gums. Just a thought that flashed through her head.

NOW, SU WAS dead. Do-kyung was gone. And there was nothing Jin-kyung could do. When she felt helpless, she thought of Ia. Jin-kyung didn't point a finger at Ia's mother like everyone else. But Jin-kyung realized after the fact that even her reasonable suspicions were an act of hostility. Knowing she wouldn't find Do-kyung at the Saha Estates, Jin-kyung went up to the park, to the pediatrician's office where Su used to work, and to the cocktail bar where Sara worked. She gazed at the heavy iron bars of the penitentiary gates. She loitered around the National Center of Gynecology and Obstetrics and the First Children's Center, the Parliament, the newspaper office, the broadcasting station. She had wandered through various parts of Town every night since the day Do-kyung went missing.

Walking back to Saha, Jin-kyung felt her right leg stiffen from the sole of her foot up to her thigh. She crouched by the vegetable garden and lit a cigarette, daunted by the flights of stairs to the seventh floor. She'd taken about two drags when she heard someone behind her. It was Ia's mother. Jin-kyung quickly stubbed her cigarette out on the ground.

"I'm sorry. I didn't see you there."

"It's okay. It's fine."

They stood standing face-to-face in the dark for a moment, then Jin-kyung bowed at her and turned to go.

"Wait," Ia's mother called.

Jin-kyung stopped and turned back. She'd never seen Ia's mother so up-close. T-shirt with the neck stretched out. Baggy shorts that came down just to her knees. She combed through her unkempt hair with her fingers, gathered it at the back, and tied it loosely with a hair elastic on her wrist. Her hair out of the way, her pale face now came into full view. Her eyes were swollen from crying, and she looked young. Jin-kyung thought they could be around the same age. She wanted to offer her words of condolence about Ia's disappearance, however belated they would be, but nothing suitable came to mind.

"Did you have something you wanted to say?" Jin-kyung said.

Looking up at Jin-kyung, Ia's mother said, "I did not sell my son. Ia. I didn't sell my Ia."

She would have been holding the words back for a long time. She wouldn't have had the chance to say them out loud. Ia's mother sniffled loudly, swallowed, and continued, "I accepted the sympathy. I accepted it thinking people were sympathetic. But once I accepted their sympathy and kindness, I couldn't raise objections about anything they did or said anymore. So now the word is I sold him. So, Jin-kyung, if people ever offer you their sympathy, don't accept it. Sympathy, kindness, care, encouragement—don't take any of it."

No. *You can accept sympathy. You can accept the sympathy and kindness people give, and it doesn't mean you can't also take issue when issues arise, or demand more when you deserve more.* Ia's singing echoed in Jin-kyung's head—the hot sun, cool breeze, that sweet nap, and the hymn woven into it all.

"I hear Ia's voice all day long," Ia's mother said, looking around. "Ia's singing. He's singing right now."

"I hear it, too. Right this moment."

Thinking Ji-kyung was just being nice, Ia's mother smiled at her awkwardly, with warmth. But it was true. Jin-kyung did hear Ia singing.

SU AND DO-KYUNG, UNIT 714

WINTER WAS WINDING DOWN. THE BREEZE IN THE HEIGHT of noon was warm but dry. The first to detect the change of season were the children, with their delicate respiratory systems. Su had many young patients waiting for her at the clinic.

Su was on her way out from seeing a child whose inner ear infection had worsened after self-medicating with small doses of cold medication for adults sold at the convenience store. When she prescribed five days' worth of antibiotics and reminded the child to take it for all five days, the kid bowed and said, enunciating every syllable, "Thank you, Doctor." There were so many sweet children at Saha. Su loved these sweet children and was upset that they were sick, but it made her happy to see them well and bubbly again. Choosing pediatrics was one of the best decisions of her life.

She was passing by the custodian's office when the old man pulled her aside to tell her there was another sick child. She followed him, thinking it was another case of the flu,

indigestion, or a stomach bug. He led her past his custodian's quarters in the back of the office, and into the bathroom.
Even as he opened the door, Su still hadn't noticed something
was amiss. She stepped into a bathroom, which was so steamy
she wondered where he found the money to afford all this hot
water. *He's probably not even paying for it, the strange old
man*, she snickered to herself.

Once she waved her arms around in big arcs to clear the
steam away, the patients came into view. Two people pushed
into a small tub together. One was skinny, with short hair, and
looked like a child at first glance, wet undershirt and panties
clinging. It was a woman. The other one was not clothed at
all. A man. Su was caught unawares, but pretended everything
was fine as she tested the temperature of the bathwater with
the back of her hand. She instructed the old man to keep filling the tub with warm water to keep the temperature up, and
opened her doctor's bag.

"It's pain medication. The pain should go away soon."

She stuck a syringe in the woman's arm first. The woman
tensed up and then let her eyes close as she relaxed. Su touched
her fingertip gently to the woman's forehead, cheek, and nose.

"This will leave a scar." Su meant to keep this thought
to herself but wound up saying it out loud anyway. She was
worried the woman would be surprised or upset by what she
said, but the woman only wheezed, staring off into nothing.
Su tried not to let her eyes wander as she gave the man an
injection as well.

"Make sure the water doesn't go cold," she told the custodian again. "I'll go get some cream and gauze from the car."

"Thanks."

Before she left for the car, she said, "Remember how I said call me only when there are children who need urgent care? If you keep doing this, I won't come anymore."

The old man flashed her a teasing smile and shrugged. "They look like children to me."

"What child is that big and hairy? And by the way, thanks for covering up the guy before bringing me in here."

The man in the tub, lying with his eyes closed as if unconscious, chuckled.

Su didn't see the man again until late fall. The zipper of his jacket was pulled all the way up to conceal half his face, but she recognized his eyes. She was going to pretend she didn't see him, but he said hello first.

"Thank you for your help."

Su couldn't think of anything to say in response.

"Aren't you the doctor who treated me and my sister that time?"

"Oh yeah . . . that's why I recognize you . . . You're okay now?"

Su's gaze kept falling to the ground as she fought to exchange polite pleasantries with the man. Concerned that she might end up doing or saying something inappropriate, she turned away before he could answer.

The man tapped on Su's shoulder twice with the tip of his finger, like knocking on a door.

"Actually, my throat is a bit scratchy these days and I have a cough. Could you have a look? Or do you only treat children?"

Sure, he was a patient, but how could he be so secure in front of someone who'd seen him completely naked? Was he really that confident? Su wondered for a moment if he had an ulterior motive.

"I'm sorry," the man said. "I shouldn't have bothered you with it."

"No, no. I was just thinking where would be a good place to take a look at your throat."

Su examined his throat in the custodian's office and checked his breathing. It was a mild case of sore throat, common at the change of seasons. Su put four days' worth of anti-inflammatory painkillers and expectorants in a box and handed it to him. All the while, the old man stood in a corner with his arms crossed and grumbled about people taking over his cramped office—how first the sister and now the brother bothered him at all hours of the day.

"I'm sorry I'm sick." The man bowed to the old man with a sincere look on his face. No trace of mockery or levity. What he was inside showed on the outside, no hidden agendas. And because of that, Su couldn't tell if he was a good person or not.

Su said goodbye to the old man and was heading out the door when the man caught back up with her.

"Thank you," he said. "For treating me and giving me meds. I have nothing to give you in return, so I'll walk you to wherever you're going."

"Oh, that's okay. I'm not scared."

"Scared? Are there scary things on the way?"

"Oh, well, I don't know. Why else would you walk me to the car?"

"It's boring if you walk by yourself. I'm not a very funny

person, but I'm good at laughing at funny stories. So why don't you tell me a funny story?"

Not offering to tell a funny story but *requesting* one. Bold or shameless? Walking side by side with the guy all the way to the park where she'd left her car, she thought about what the old man had told her about him. He had killed a man. He stabbed the man responsible for his mother's death multiple times with a huge weapon. Was it seven or eight times? Su thought he didn't *seem* like a bad person, but that didn't necessarily mean he wasn't capable of killing. It didn't make sense, but she understood; a person who could kill someone responsible for his mother's death. A kind, guileless person who killed another person. These qualities that seemed mismatched somehow fit together to make this straightforward man who he was.

He said his name was Do-kyung. When they reached Su's car, he bowed as he had to the old man earlier and said goodbye. Su was sorry to see him go.

"Do you want a ride back to Saha?"

"No, I'm going for a walk. Nothing to do back home anyway."

"Then do you want to go for a walk with me?"

Do-kyung gazed at Su in silence.

"You asked for a funny story," Su added sheepishly. "I didn't get to tell you one."

Walking up the dirt path together, Su told him all kinds of stories as they came to mind. Stories of her little patients' cute antics, her family, the movie she saw over the weekend, and so on. Do-kyung didn't laugh as promised.

"I thought you said you were good at laughing at funny stories."

"Your stories are not that funny."

Su laughed. After this, Su came by to treat Saha children more frequently and always went for a walk with Do-kyung afterward.

SU CAME UP with the idea of living together. Do-kyung couldn't make sense of what she was suggesting.

"With what money? If someone rats me out, I'll get banished back here."

"I'm moving in with you."

"What?"

"I'm on a salary. You think I've saved enough to buy a place? And by the way, if someone rats you out, you don't end up back here. You get thrown in the ocean."

"So you'd live in Saha? Why?"

Su looked squarely at Do-kyung. "Because I want to live with you."

Getting a unit assigned wouldn't be a big deal; Do-kyung was an adult, and he hadn't caused any problems with the other residents. He wasn't worried about the process or qualifications. But he doubted Su would be able to live with the inconvenience and uncertainty that came with life in the Saha Estates.

"You know we get electricity from the solar panels on the roof, right? We hardly get enough, and there are blackouts all the time. We can't afford heating and cooling. We don't even have plumbing in the units. We have to wash and cook with the water from the yard, and if we want hot water we have to heat it ourselves on a gas burner. It's going to be completely different from where you live now. It's cold, it's hot, it's dirty. So if you live with me, you'll begin to hate it here, and then you won't like me, either."

"Look into getting a generator. The type you charge or the type with a crank, either's fine. Something with good capacity. And let's get a water tank. We'll do some construction so that we can get water in the bathroom and kitchen. We can install a water heater in the bathroom. Getting one for the kitchen will be expensive and take up a lot of electricity, so we'll work on that later. You'll do the dishes with rubber gloves on. And make sure the water level in the tank isn't low. And we'll have the unit insulated. I don't have money to buy a place, but I have enough for basic home improvement. It'll be the best unit in Saha."

"But don't you think the others will, um, I don't know, frown upon it? If we're the only ones fixing it up and making it fancy?"

"How is that fancy? Plumbing and heating and cooling? That's just the basics. You don't have to keep living like this, you know. We'll move in together and fix things one at a time. If we do it, others will follow."

Su was right. She wasn't pressuring Do-kyung, but Do-kyung felt uncomfortable all the same.

"If you've been living here with nothing and there's nothing you can do about it, it's hard to think that way. We don't live like this because we're dumb or lazy."

"So you need someone like me. I have a lot, there's lots I can do, and I like you."

To install the water tank on the roof, they had to live on

the top floor. Do-kyung suggested moving right next door to Jin-kyung, and Su said, "Are you insane?"

Do-kyung and Su chose Unit 714, the farthest from Jin-kyung's.

The unit was renovated according to Su's plan. The ceiling and walls received waterproofing treatment and were reinforced with insulation. They wallpapered the living room and bedroom in different colors. The kitchen was too small for a dining table, so they agreed to put a floor table by the window and use it as a place to eat, have tea, and read. They put a mattress in the bedroom, and had cupboards custom-made to fit the foyer, bathroom, and veranda. Shelves were installed all around the living room. Books, pictures, a radio, and dishes were kept on the shelves, and when they ran out of room, extra books were stacked on the floor.

A fine white layer of dust settled everywhere as they made holes in the walls and ceilings to renovate. Do-kyung's first task of the day was to fetch water from the yard and fill the roof water tank halfway. When he lived with Jin-kyung, they used about two to four containers' worth per day. Filling the entire water tank on the roof required sixteen, but he didn't bother filling it all the way up. He wiped the apartment down with a wet rag all morning. The windowsills, the thresholds, and the inside of the kitchen sink kept accumulating dust in spite of the diligent cleaning. When Do-kyung showed signs of getting fed up, Su said they didn't have to make the apartment spotless before moving in. She said like it was nothing: "The dust will clear up once we begin to live in the space—running our hands on surfaces and moving the air as we come and go."

Do-kyung wanted to give Su a present to welcome her to the Saha Estates. He sketched a design to make her a bookcase and a bookstand. Then he looked into acquiring wood and carpentry tools, which were more than he could afford. Do-kyung couldn't manage to make anything beyond the design he drew, and felt incompetent and depressed. When he shared this with Su, she said she would like the design as a present.

"I don't have that many books, and I'm so sick and tired of studying at this point. I don't need a bookcase."

With the design for a bookcase and a built-in folding bookstand as her moving-in gift, Su became a resident of Saha Estates, Building A, Unit 714.

THE OLD LADY at the temp agency called Do-kyung a few times, but he refused to answer, as he was busy getting the apartment tidied up. The old agent asked very seriously if he was intending to starve himself to death, which worried Do-kyung, but Su suggested such work really wasn't necessary now.

"I make enough money for the both of us. Our place requires more upkeep than the average house, so how about you focus on maintaining it? And don't you like to draw? How about doing something with that? Your design was good."

Su didn't even know what kind of drawing Do-kyung did. And she'd complimented his design without being able to tell good design from bad. Do-kyung laughed out loud with his mouth wide open. A serious look came over him again, then he chuckled to himself.

"Draw for what?"

"Just start drawing. I'll make sure you find a use for it."

Su led Do-kyung by the hand to an old art supplies district by the university and bought paper, oils, brushes, pencils, and erasers. Su paid for it all. Do-kyung arranged the art supplies in the spot he'd reserved for Su's bookcase and declared in a state of delirious excitement that his first drawing would be a gift to Su. Su begged him not to do a portrait of her, but he did exactly that. He used big dollops of oils and his brushstrokes were carefree. Su, who knew nothing about art, wished he would use the oils sparingly.

She framed the painting and hung it in her office at work. None of the features were Su's, but it was unmistakably her no matter who she asked. The painting had a magnetism. After seeing it, some of her coworkers commissioned paintings, and Su passed on their photos to Do-kyung. Soon it became a trend, all the doctors had a painting by Do-kyung hanging on their walls. The pharmaceutical reps and guardians of sick children also commissioned portraits. Su suggested putting an ad in the paper. Do-kyung wasn't sure it was a good idea.

"Wouldn't I have to report the income to the Revenue Service or something? And how would I get compensated? I can't even open a bank account."

"It'll be okay if you start small. If the business grows big enough that you need to register, we'll worry about it then. In the meantime, you can use my account."

"I don't feel comfortable using your account."

"It's not like you're raking in the dough. It won't be a problem. If someone asks, I'll say I'm the painter. I'll tell them I'm a good painter."

"No, I mean . . . will you show me the bank statements?"

"Hey! I won't steal your money!"

A small flyer went up on the hospital bulletin board and at the apartment complex nearby.

People at Saha also started commissioning paintings from time to time. It wasn't much, but Do-kyung had an income again. Su printed out the order list and the transactions monthly to have Do-kyung look it over. Su started asking around for galleries that would display work from unknown artists, and Do-kyung started branching out from portraits to other subjects.

THE HEAD OF the pediatrician's office had a grim look. Su tugged at the hem of her sleeves, not knowing what to say.

"How long has this been going on? When the hell did it begin? Did you steal from our supplies? Did you steal our meds?" As she interrogated Su, she tapped on the desk with her index finger.

"But—"

"No. I don't want to hear it. I don't want to hear your excuses."

Su didn't get to finish her sentence. Not that she would have been able to say the words out loud, given the opportunity: "But you knew, Doctor. You knew what I was up to."

Su's office was the only one that was always low on gauze, disinfectants, and disposable tongue compressors. An administrative staff member had complained about it outright during a meeting, and the chief physician chided the team, instructing them to do two things: "Take your time with the examination and get the diagnosis right. And make sure the exam room is stocked with supplies." A few days later, the chief physician sent up some extra pain and fever meds and antibiotics.

There had been a baby at Saha with a burn. Just twelve months old, the baby had toddled over to a floor table and knocked over an electric kettle. When Su arrived, Granny Konnim was cooling the affected area with cold water next to the mother, who was too scared to even touch her baby. Su disinfected the wound, applied cream, bandaged the area, and left with a heavy heart. The burn wasn't so bad, but it was wide and the baby was too young. Most importantly, there had been difficulties communicating with the baby's mother.

The following afternoon, Granny Konnim called. The mother had undone the bandage because the baby was getting impatient. The blisters chafed and popped, and Granny Konnim was in a panic. If the area was infected, the treatment could get complicated. She asked Granny Konnim to bring the baby by after seven in the evening when the hospital would be empty. Su was tense for the rest of the day. Around seven, the chief physician, who happened to be the last one to leave that day, came by Su's office and patted her on the shoulder.

"I'm off. *Keep up . . . the good work.*"

Then she walked over to the window, closed the blinds, and slowly walked out of the exam room. A signal, a code. Su felt that the chief physician's every word, gesture, look, and even the way she breathed had footnotes on them. The dry hand that patted her on the shoulder, the way she said, *Keep up the good work*, the blind that closed soundlessly, her slow footsteps out of the exam room. Su could read the meaning behind them, and was sure of her interpretations.

Su lost her medical license permanently for practicing medicine beyond the scope her license permitted. The investigator looked back and forth between a stack of documents and Su, and asked Su for her address. She wondered why he was asking when it was all there in the paperwork, but gave him her parents' address anyway.

The investigator snickered at her. "Are you sure you live there?"

"Yes."

"I was just checking."

Then he shook his head and muttered, "Why do this to yourself?" Su wondered the same thing, *Seriously, why do this to myself?*

IN MIDDLE SCHOOL, there was a smelly girl in Su's class. It was just body odor, the musty smell of sweaty underarms. The girl was quiet and kind. She didn't ever start conversations, cause any trouble, or speak ill of others. If not for the smell, no one would have noticed her presence. Perhaps she had tried to have as little presence as possible because of the odor. A fishy, pungent smell wafted over on the gentle breeze coming in through the windows, but it was not unbearable. Even the most immature middle school kids refrained from calling her smelly.

One day, the first period had just begun when the girl had a nosebleed. The word *nosebleed* didn't begin to describe the amount of blood gushing from her nose like a late summer downpour. The dark red blood fell onto the front of her very thin white uniform blouse. The kid sitting next to her screamed bloody murder. The girl seemed more frightened by the screaming and the commotion she was causing than by the actual bleeding.

Her shirt was an unsalvageable mess, but she didn't have anything to change into. The teacher said, "Anyone have a gym shirt?" No one answered. Most left their gym clothes in their lockers and wore them several times between washings, so it was unlikely anyone had a shirt that would be useful. The kids thought that the smell was contagious. Among classmates who turned their heads and tried to not meet her eyes, the girl bit her lower lip and looked like she was about to cry.

"I have one," Su said.

She walked over to her locker in the back of the classroom and pulled out her gym shirt. The next day, Su got her shirt back freshly laundered and smelling good, but the incident did not bring the two girls together.

Young Su had also thought that the smell was contagious, and that she might have to throw the shirt out. She was anxious and upset. At the same time, she had not pitied the girl, and wasn't even trying to comfort her; a classmate simply needed a shirt to change into, and Su had one. An uncomplicated, natural conclusion that contained no kindness, a gesture that had no calculation behind it.

SU KEPT HER spirits up after her license was revoked. She said that it didn't mean all her skills and knowledge disappeared with it, and in all seriousness floated the idea of starting a clinic at Saha. She looked into getting medical supplies and medication through pharmaceutical companies, which turned out to be a challenge. She tried asking college friends with practices to help out. The friends who hadn't heard what had happened to her asked what was going on. Su tried telling the truth at first, then started to beat around the bush, or dodge the question with a joke. Then she stopped responding to the question altogether. Su went to visit her parents and didn't return for over a week.

Meanwhile, Do-kyung painted alone in the house. He ate three meals a day and when night fell washed his hair, the back of his ears, his armpits, and between his toes with the warm water from the bathroom water heater; he slept under the covers that dried in the sun during the day. But on the third day alone, he knocked on Jin-kyung's door. Jin-kyung didn't say a thing as she handed him a damp pillow from the closet. Do-kyung rolled over on his side with his back to Jin-kyung and cried a little. He didn't cry from the next day onward, but he did continue going to Jin-kyung's to sleep.

On the morning of the tenth day, Su came up the stairs to the seventh floor with both hands full of paper bags and plastic grocery bags. A long stalk of spring onion stuck out from one; Do-kyung liked how Su could look like something out of a movie in moments like these. His worries and resentment melted away. In the paper bag was a T-shirt, light summer shorts, and a new pair of sneakers she'd bought for him, and the grocery bag contained a big slab of beef, fresh eggplants, carrots, mushrooms, and all sorts of condiments, from salt and pepper to other spices to sauces Do-kyung had never seen in his life.

"Let's have a barbecue. Go get Jin-kyung, too. I bought lots so we can share," were the first words out of Su's mouth.

Do-kyung was upset that Su was so cheerful, acting as if nothing had happened.

"No," Do-kyung said.

"Okay, then we'll have all the meat to ourselves."

Do-kyung put the portable stove on the table and fried the meat, onion, eggplants, carrots, and mushrooms all together in a large frying pan. Su was not at all interested in the vegetables, and gorged on the meat that leaked blood as she picked up pieces with her fork. "I've really been craving meat, I haven't had meat in such a long time, a person's gotta eat meat," she murmured to herself as she ate, even though the meat wasn't that good. The pretty folds of marbling stank of dead flesh.

Her mouth full, Su talked about her plans to look for research positions at hospitals, schools, or research centers. She had been busy looking for jobs and sending in materials for applications.

"I kept you waiting, didn't I?"

"I was worried."

"About what? That something happened to me, or that I'd run away?"

"Both."

"Which one did you worry about more?"

"The latter."

Su laughed. She worried that she didn't have anything to wear to an interview, but no place she applied to requested one. Su got in the habit of saying things to herself like, "Should I go back to school? Should I move to the mainland? Should I start over with a different major?"

The misfortune did not end. The pediatrician's office where she used to work was under investigation and the chief physi-

cian was held suspect. When the practice came under threat
of being closed down, the chief physician filed a suit against
Su for tortious interference and embezzlement. Depending on
the outcome of the trial, Su could lose her citizenship. And
that would affect her family as well. Su unraveled. Do-kyung
understood. She had been brave and cheerful for long enough.

SU CAME UP with the idea. She also chose the parking lot by
the park as their final place together.

Muted light from a faraway streetlight filtered in through
the car windows. Su sat up and kissed Do-kyung, who was
having second thoughts, on the neck, and only then did Do-
kyung let go of everything. Su placed in Do-kyung's palm a
round white pill, an oblong pink pill, and a capsule containing
a yellow liquid.

"Don't worry. It'll be like falling asleep."

And in her own hand, Su placed the capsule and the same
two pills she gave Do-kyung, plus two other pills. When Do-
kyung seized Su's wrist in surprise, Su slowly freed herself
from Do-kyung's grasp.

"I have to take more than my usual dosage."

"What if something happens to you?"

Su laughed. "That's the whole point."

The realization and sadness made Do-kyung laugh as
well. He should have taken the same dosage she had. But it
was too late for regrets.

DO-KYUNG HAD MADE up his mind to leave Sara's.

Before heading to work on that day, Sara put a wooden
spoon on the dining table and bade him, "Eat quietly with

this. When you're done, don't put anything away. Don't wash your hands, and don't flush. Just sleep. Go to bed early."

Do-kyung thought two nights and two days had come and gone since he began hiding at Sara's, but he couldn't be sure. The police had stormed Saha suddenly, and Do-kyung ended up in the small, cold fridge like a piece of meat, in the same cotton pants bloodied and torn at the knees. It wasn't too cold in the fridge, but his teeth chattered. When he felt the sound of his teeth chattering was louder than the hum of the motor, he clenched his jaw hard.

As a boy, Do-kyung was so terrified of the dark basement room where his father lay like a corpse that he couldn't eat or do his homework. All he could do was cry as he waited for Jin-kyung to come home. Following the sound of her brother crying from down the street, Jin-kyung would run in after school and scold him for sitting in the dark and crying like a baby instead of turning the light on, but Do-kyung couldn't tell her that he couldn't reach the light switch.

Su had cried just as Do-kyung did when he was a child—bursts of sobs heaving out, tears streaming down her face. Do-kyung picked up the wooden spoon, then put it down. *Su,* he thought. *Is she really dead?*

Do-kyung went over to the veranda, held a corner of the curtain in his hand, pulled it toward him, and let go. The window happened to be open and the curtain billowed naturally, as if it were blowing in the gentle night breeze. Through the curtains, Do-kyung saw flashes of the night scene. Beyond the alley so narrow a car could hardly squeeze through, the back of a commercial building came into view: wall grimy from streaks of rain, bathroom window, fire escape, air-conditioning fans . . . The commercial district, built without proper planning, wound up with many narrow passageways wide enough for children to bolt around but difficult for adults to navigate. These paths ran along low walls and led to the occasional side entrance.

The sound of shutters rolling down and tired voices bidding farewell until tomorrow rang from below. Those dark, hidden, deserted alleys. Do-kyung thought it was worth a shot.

The potato soup on the dining table had gone cold and formed a sticky film. The rice ball made of orange fish roe and laver bits was also hard on the surface. Do-kyung fetched the milk from the fridge and poured himself a big glass. When he couldn't chew on the rice ball anymore, he had a spoonful of potato soup, and when that didn't help the rice ball go down, he took a sip of milk. Worried he might get indigestion from eating for the first time after starving for so long, he chewed every bite so thoroughly he could feel the grains of rice mushed on his tongue. He finished everything Sara had prepared for him. He moved the empty plates to the sink, thought about doing the dishes, and after a pause, left them.

He took out the sneakers he'd hidden deep in the freezer in a black plastic bag, placed them under the curtains, and stretched—first his neck and shoulders, then his wrists, waist, knees, and all the way down to his ankles. He gently loosened his joints by rolling them, then massaged his thighs and calves with the balls of his hands. He could tell that his muscles were weak.

The sneakers were cold and stiff. He tried jumping in place. He landed hard after the first jump and felt the shock of it go straight to the floor, but he recovered the sensation in his legs over a few more jumps and was able to land soundlessly using the elasticity of his feet, ankles, and knees.

Leaning against the wall, Do-kyung mapped out the escape route in his head. Curtains, veranda, first floor, road, park, the coastal road . . . *And then I could run along the coast or jump into the ocean. I will go where a path opens up. I might have to cross the border again. I'm not afraid. I can't hide in Sara's refrigerator forever.*

He took a deep breath and stood at the window, listening. He heard a metal door fly open and slam shut, and a high-pitched scream—he couldn't tell if it was coming from a woman or a man. The fear and anxiety he had pushed deep down rose up again. His heart was pounding. He tried to get it together. The ruckus in Saha was perhaps an opportunity for him to get out.

Do-kyung gently lifted the red and yellow tulip-print curtains and jumped out into the veranda. The important thing at this stage was to get out of Saha without injury. He opened the window and bug screen as wide as they would go, held tight on to the top of the window frame, swung over to the other side of the railing, and lowered himself by hanging on to the bottom bar of the railing. He landed softly on the ground by bending his knees at the appropriate time, so he didn't make a thud or hurt his joints. Another long scream rang out somewhere in Saha, and a few windows lit up. Do-kyung quickly hopped over the wall.

DO-KYUNG STOOD FACING the four-lane road he'd crossed the night of Su's death. It was far enough away from downtown and close to midnight, so there weren't many cars. But the few cars and motorcycles that did go by zipped through as if to tear the fabric of the wind. On the other side of the road was the park Do-kyung had run from. *That night, I dashed across the street from there to here. Without looking. I guess I was that desperate to live. Or die.*

A motorcycle flew by with a roar that shook the ground, and then a baffling silence fell. A set of careless footsteps came toward Do-kyung. He flinched, ready to duck, but stopped himself in order not to make himself conspicuous. The footsteps stopped. Do-kyung pivoted and ran in the opposite direction.

When he reached an alley between the old, low commercial and office buildings, a woman saw him and collapsed on the spot, shrieking. Do-kyung ran past the woman, jumped over a railing, knocked over a large garbage bag, and ran without looking back. The smell of blood rose up from his throat.

Do-kyung chose the narrowest, most dirty, and dangerous paths at every turn. A stampede of footsteps came after him and fell away, then cautious, quiet footsteps drew near and grew distant. As he jumped over a metal gate, Do-kyung's leg caught on a bar that left a deep laceration on his knee. The already bloodstained pants leg tore off and his white bone showed through the gaping wound. *Not the right leg again.* Do-kyung sat against the wall with his hands around his knee. He clenched his jaw to swallow a scream, and heard the latch of the metal gate squeak. He jumped to his feet and ran again.

The electric pain shooting up his knee and thigh made it impossible to speed up. He turned around and saw a well-built man in cotton pants and cotton shirt, hair so completely white it was hard to tell his age, jumping over the metal gate in one agile motion. Do-kyung climbed the fire escape in front of him. It was a rickety fire escape that went up the side of the building in a zigzag. He couldn't see where it ended. The stairs squeaked noisily.

Do-kyung clung to the metal and crawled his way up one step at a time. The man followed him, keeping a distance. Do-kyung arrived at the last step. With nowhere else to go, he tried the door into the building. It did not move. Then he looked down. He was maybe five stories up. The footsteps pursuing him suddenly picked up speed and the fire escape swung wildly. With no time to lose, Do-kyung grabbed the railing and leaned out as though about to jump when the man shouted from below.

"STOP!"

On that cue, the door to the building flew open and a young man jumped out. He aimed a pistol at Do-kyung's temple and said in a hushed voice, "Don't die."

Do-kyung froze.

"Weren't you going to jump?" the man jeered. "Too scared to die, huh?"

The man with the full head of white hair came up the last step, twisted Do-kyung's arm around his back, and forced him to kneel. Do-kyung was awash with shame—he had failed himself and Su. Tears welled up in his eyes. The barrel of the pistol poked him on the head.

"Why did you kill her?"

Do-kyung kept silent.

"*Why! Why! Why did you kill her!*"

The young man unleashed his outrage at Do-kyung as if Su were his family. The utterly personal emotional response of the young man hinted that assumptions had already formed around Town regarding Su's death. Heavy tears fell from Do-kyung's eyes.

"*I DID NOT KILL HER!*"

PEOPLE WERE CURIOUS to know if the incident was a love scandal or a crime. *Titillated* might be more accurate. Of the two people who knew the truth, one was dead and the other was unreliable. But there were definitely those who remembered Do-kyung and Su as a couple. The news ran an interview with one of Su's coworkers, who reported that she saw them eating together at a restaurant by the hospital, and an interview with a café owner who remembered the two of them coming by sometimes and gazing at each other without saying much.

"Not many people pay cash these days. That's why I remembered him. He always ordered a beer, and the doctor always ordered coffee. And the man always paid cash. So I wondered for a moment if he was a Saha, but my kid's doctor was also at that hospital. I thought no way a doctor like that would go out with a Saha. So I was shocked when I found out."

"Did they look like lovers? Was there any indication that the man was dragging the woman around?"

"I actually got the impression the man was on a tight leash.

Oh, and this one time, the doctor slammed her hands down on the table, got up, and left by herself. So the man pulled out a bunch of cash from his pocket to pay the bill, and followed her out."

"Without taking the change?"

"No, he took all the change."

Despite the number of eyewitness accounts, the world did not accept Su and Do-kyung as an average couple. Common sense was more convincing than firsthand accounts. The man was not even an L2 but a complete Saha, and the woman was a Town pediatrician. Speculations suggested she had something to hide or feared for her life.

The media dug into Su's past and reported that her parents had divorced when she was very young, that she lived with a stepmother for over twenty years, that her engagement to a man eleven years her senior was broken right before the wedding, and that she received plastic surgery after that. People came up with all sorts of theories to understand Su's decisions, but no one could make sense of her. A relationship was, after all, between the two people involved, a world with its own private rules.

Unofficially the greatest scandal in the history of Town. Officially a Saha male raping and murdering a Citizen female. In the end, Do-kyung could not protect Su from being passed around as the protagonist of vulgar gossip, and no amount of struggle could get Do-kyung out of the snare he was caught in. While the rest of Town thought they had Su all figured out, Do-kyung would always think of Su as a wonder.

EUNJIN, UNIT 305. THIRTY YEARS EARLIER.

A new strain of infectious respiratory disease had spread worldwide. Apart from speculations that it was communicable through saliva, nothing was revealed about its cause or cure. Healthy people suffered from cold-like symptoms that cleared in a couple weeks, but for those with weak respiratory systems or preexisting conditions it was fatal. The elderly, the pregnant, and babies were especially vulnerable. The fatality rate in the first area of outbreak was over forty percent, and pregnant women who contracted the disease miscarried without exception, regardless of what trimester they were in. The fate of humanity itself rested on the outcome of the pandemic.

Town had very little contact with the rest of the world, and its people could not travel overseas freely. So Town alone was insulated from the worldwide panic. No one had to wash their hands thoroughly, wear masks, or be vigilant about not coughing on others. They only heard about the symptoms of patients overseas on the news, and shook their heads as they sat back and tracked the rising death toll. *Why can't they cure a disease? What has the world come to?*

THE CHILD'S BREATH had turned raspy on a Friday night. On the small side for a four-year-old, he kept tossing and turning in his struggle to breathe, and wound up rolling all the way over to the built-in closet in the corner of the bedroom. Curled up in the crawling position, he panted and struggled like a dying bug and broke into fits of dry cough.

He was known to be susceptible to minor illnesses, which led the caregivers to dismiss this as another cold. The sun was warm, and the air was clean and not too dry after the recent spring showers. They were expecting this turn of season to be uneventful. Only Eunjin, the contract caregiver, thought something was off.

The child's condition grew worse over the weekend. The medical staff and the senior caregivers at the orphanage had the weekend off, so Eunjin administered meds from the first-aid kit. She gave him barley tea and rice porridge, put a scarf around his neck, and held him all day as he fussed in agony and tried to fight off whatever he had. His cheeks flushed, the child fell asleep in Eunjin's arms with his mouth open. He woke up and cried, then fell asleep again. Eunjin's arms felt ready to fall off from holding the child all day. The other caregivers complained that she was giving all her attention to one child, who was only getting worse despite her efforts, and the flustered Eunjin wanted to cry along with him.

Eunjin had once been a child in the orphanage herself. In the wake of Town's independence, many native residents went missing, and even more children were abandoned; and Eunjin had been one of them. She was twelve at the time.

When Eunjin was living in the orphanage, a younger girl in her room got her right hand caught in a door. She broke her pinkie and ring fingers, and had to have her fingers in a cast and her hand in protective gear. Unfortunately, the girl was right-handed. At mealtimes, every bite required a battle of will with her chopsticks. She placed the chopsticks along her left thumb and forefinger in an X, put the piece of tofu or

meat between the chopsticks, and gently squeezed her hand.
The food flew off her plate almost every time. She couldn't
do more than push it around on the flat surface of the plate
with her spoon. Eunjin saw this and placed food on the girl's
spoon. She fed her, clothed her, and washed her hair. Eunjin
had always been caring. She often held the younger girls who
shared a room with her, braided their hair, and folded back
the sleeves that came down to the tips of their fingers.

"You should be a caregiver when you grow up," said the
head caregiver in passing as she watched her proudly, and the
words stuck with Eunjin.

Eunjin assumed that life after the orphanage was predes-
tined, like water flowing from high to low, flowers blooming
in the spring, and sweat pouring under the hot sun. When she
"grew up"—meaning when she turned seventeen and had to
leave the orphanage—she would simply live out the rest of her
days until a fatal accident or disease took her life. That was all
there was for an L2. Work details were assigned to them; they
didn't get to dream or have a say in their futures. But the head
caregiver's passing comment changed Eunjin.

Orphaned children started job training at fifteen. They
spent one year sampling various jobs, from driving and simple
electrical work to cooking, and their second year was spent
focusing and apprenticing in one field. The children were
assigned to their respective fields at random; they didn't have
a say, nor did the teacher take the children's preferences into
consideration.

On Eunjin's fifteenth birthday, she went to see the head
caregiver.

"I should be a caregiver," she said.

The head caregiver took a long look at Eunjin and asked her why.

"You said so. 'You should be a caregiver when you grow up.' You said that last year."

"You can work at a home. In the kitchen or as a cleaning staff. But caregiver is not a job option for an L2."

"I know, but you said, 'You should be a caregiver when you grow up.' You said that anyway. You did."

The head caregiver pulled up a chair from the corner of her office and sat Eunjin down.

"I know you," she explained as she looked Eunjin in the eye. "You are kind and hardworking, and you're good at reading people. You like children and you're considerate. Some kids are good with their hands, others are good with words or good with details . . . it's such a waste of talent, it's pathetic, to assign work like randomly drawing cards. I'll try."

Eunjin was assigned to food preparation. She got herself a few food-preparation-related certificates over the course of her training year, apprenticed in the kitchen at the home, and left the home as an L2 on her seventeenth birthday. When the younger kids cried and clung to her as she was about to leave, she gave them each a hug and promised she would come back, that she would come back as a caregiver.

Eunjin turned down the kitchen staff position she was offered through the home. The job was at the university cafeteria, just about the best position a graduate of the home could hope for, but Eunjin believed she would become a caregiver, and was willing to wait for the opportunity. In the meantime, she needed a place to live. So she went to the Saha Estates.

AT THE RESIDENT interview, Eunjin said slowly but clearly
that she had L2 status, a certificate as a food preparation spe-
cialist, that she was waiting to be a caregiver, which was what
she really wanted to do, that she liked children and was good
at looking after them, and that she could look after the children at Saha. The corners of her mouth twitched as she spoke.
She was embarrassed and worried about the impression she.
was giving when Queen Grandma reached over and patted
Eunjin on the head.

"We're not testing you," she said. "Or grading you. What
your skills are or what certificates you have are not important
to us, and besides, we don't know what they mean anyway.
This is a meet-and-greet to see if you'll be okay living here
with us, if you'll fit in here."

Eunjin became the first resident of Unit 305, which had
been unoccupied. She cleaned and wiped every corner of the
apartment for a long time. She threw all the doors and windows open, and scrubbed and polished all day long as other
residents joked that she would polish her apartment off the
face of the earth.

During the day when the sun was out, she played in the
yard with the children. Eunjin knew a lot of games they could
play by drawing on the ground with chalk. They tossed pebbles on numbered squares and hopped from one square to the
next to retrieve the pebbles, leapt from circle to circle, made
tunnels out of a sequence of triangles, squares, and circles.
Eunjin's game ideas were endless. The children clamored
around her, shouting, "Again! Again! Another! Another!"
And Eunjin would pick up her chalk and make another game
appear like magic.

On rainy days, Eunjin gathered the children at Queen Grandma's place and they played with scraps of paper. If they found a piece of paper that wasn't torn, she folded it many times and cut the corners in various shapes with a pair of scissors. When opened, the cut corners transformed into wondrous shapes that repeated. The children gasped—*Wow!* The small square pieces were folded into birds, turtles, puppies, and frogs. The younger kids gathered the paper animals into a paper zoo, and the older kids learned how to fold animals and supplied the zoo with an endless population.

The very worn-down and tattered pieces of paper were soaked in water to make plaster. They stuck the plaster on balloons blown up to the size of a face, laid strips of plaster on one side, made holes for eyes and nose, and dried it to make a mask. One day to plaster the balloon, one day to decorate, and then they had a mask to play with. The children could entertain themselves for days with the same recycled paper.

In this depressing place of exile, children were a burden and an inconvenience that had to be put up with. The children in the Estates noticed the way the adults looked at them. But when Eunjin arrived, Saha transformed into a new place for the children; they learned what it was like to look forward to something. They could hope that something fun would happen tomorrow. The mother of the twins in Unit 304 thanked Eunjin when they finally met on the walkway.

"The kids are eating so well these days," she said.

Eunjin never cooked or fed the children or taught them table manners, but everyone knew that the reason they were eating better was thanks to Eunjin.

While Eunjin was spending her days with the children at Saha, the head caregiver at the home worked hard to keep her promise. Knowing it was almost impossible for an individual to change the job placement system, she kept bringing it up as an issue. Once the subject was brought up in a public forum, many other teachers and caregivers backed her up. The head caregiver also continued to argue that caregiver positions should be open to L2s. Because caregivers had to be assigned around the clock, they worked eight-hour shifts. It wasn't hard to sell the idea that the home needed extra manpower for the sake of caregivers' welfare and keeping the home running smoothly, but whether L2s were qualified to take on the task was a whole other discussion. The home decided to test this idea by using Eunjin as an example. She became a two-year contract caregiver.

It had been a long wait. But when Eunjin received the news she'd been waiting for, she couldn't leap for joy. Would Saha children continue to have good appetites without her around? She went to the home to sign the contract and move her things in without having completely made up her mind, and saw the head caregiver bursting with excitement.

"I do hope you do well here. For you and for me, and for the children who'll be growing up here."

Between the joy of finally being able to do what she wanted and the guilt of leaving the children of Saha, Eunjin felt a sense of responsibility rising up inside her: she could be a turning point.

Eunjin bought a spiral-bound notebook, sketched the eighteen games she had drawn in the yard at Saha, and added simple game instructions. In the remaining pages, she drew in folding instructions for paper animals. When Queen Grandma received the notebook, she turned over a few pages, said the writing was too small for her to read, and asked her to leave it in the custodian's office where everyone could look at it. The broad-shouldered custodian seemed a bit embarrassed when Eunjin caught him hunched over in his office deep in concentration over a piece of folded paper he was cutting to make shapes. Eunjin taught him different ways to fold the paper—how to make radial shapes, repeating patterns, a long strip, with thick paper, with thin paper, and so forth. She drew shapes to go with different types of paper and folding methods. The custodian nodded and listened intently.

She promised the children at Saha that she would come visit. She'd promised the kids at the home, and she'd kept the first promise. She was confident she'd be able to keep the second as well.

EUNJIN WAS ALWAYS the first caregiver to figure out why babies were crying. She was the best at understanding babies whose pronunciations were unclear, the first to notice sleeves that were too short and shoes with worn-out soles; she was the one adolescents opened up to. Her contract was renewed after two years. She discovered through keen-eyed observation that a child she was looking after had something far more serious than a cold. She became the second recorded case of the new respiratory disease in Town; the child turned out to be patient zero.

The child was brought to the home after he was born

three years ago, and he'd never left the facility in his life. The only people he'd come into contact with the month before he got sick were the seven boys that he shared a room with, five caregivers, two of the mealtime staff, and one pediatrician. There was no way he could have contracted the disease if not through the adults coming and going, so it was clear the disease had already been in Town, but the child was officially recorded as Town's patient zero.

The boy's roommates, all ages three to four, soon tested positive for the disease. The eight children and Eunjin were quarantined in an emergency facility in the home; the rest of it was shut down. Eunjin looked after the children. She had no choice. The sick children demanded care more desperately than ever, but the non-L2 staff were banned due to the high risk, and the medical staff administered only the basic treatment and quickly cleared out. There was no cure anyway. All the medical staff could do were three things: run tests, quarantine, and lift quarantine.

Spring came slowly that year. Warm rays of sun shone one day, then biting-cold gusts of wind came the next, and the boughs bearing fresh buds were snapped under the weight of heavy snow. The infected children spent the entire spring in the room. At the first sign of symptoms receding, they drew pictures, played ball games, and danced around with the intravenous lines connected to pain medication and nutrition bags still in their arms. They drew each other's faces, the windows and curtains, and the trees and clouds.

To thank the children for their portraits, Eunjin drew them a rabbit. The children asked what it was.

"Oh, you've never seen one." Eunjin raised her hands up to her head and wiggled them like ears, and hopped around like a rabbit. The children still looked puzzled.

One child pointed to the rabbit ears in the drawing and said, "Are these hands?"

Where to start, with children who spent their entire lives in the home, and all of spring in this emergency facility? The children looked up at her wide-eyed, waiting for an answer. Eunjin explained that they were ears, not hands. There's an animal with large ears that hops around. And the animal is called a rabbit.

Eunjin contacted the off-site kitchen via the intercom and requested picture cards from the children's library along with their next meal. When it arrived, she used the picture cards to teach the children the names of animals big and small that lived in the mountains, birds that flew in the sky, flowers, fruits. When the rabbit card came up, the children cheered wildly.

She told them about the sun. *It rises and sets. The moon rises and sets. The moon changes shape every day. When the rain stops, a rainbow appears. There are four seasons. After spring comes summer, after summer comes fall, after fall comes winter, and after winter comes the warm spring, when buds come in, leaves sprout, and flowers bloom. The tree outside the window is a cherry tree, and it will soon be full of light pink flowers.* The kids were still too young to understand, but one of them who was listening to Eunjin's every word looked out the window. The little snowflakes fell slowly as the wind carried them across the pane, and tears fell from the boy's eyes.

"Why won't spring come?"

"It's March now and spring begins in March. So the snow should have melted by now. It's being a slowpoke, but when it leaves, spring will really come."

"I don't think it will ever stop snowing. But I think I will stop breathing."

Eunjin was overcome with a sorrow words could not describe. Choking back tears, she asked, "Are you sad?"

"I'm scared."

The child died before the cherry blossoms came in. Eunjin wondered for a moment how things would have turned out differently had she not left Saha Estates. The new respiratory disease took one-sixth of the children at the home and two of the L2 staff. Eunjin was one of them.

ONE MONTH EARLIER, the physician in charge of infants and toddlers at the home took two days off to attend a seminar. Foreign medical staff were invited. A few people at the seminar showed symptoms of the new respiratory disease, but they were not officially recorded as cases. The routes they took, the people they came in contact with, and the medical facilities they visited all fell under classified information. Releasing too much information could bring widespread chaos to society and put medical staff—who were already working hard to fight the epidemic—at a disadvantage.

Establishments largely for L2s—children's homes, workplaces, dormitories—were locked down the moment someone was suspected of carrying the virus. A lot of the time, those who were not infected were quarantined as well. The ones who survived were able to survive without help, and in the following spring when the last patient who happened to be an L2 died, Town declared the outbreak over.

GRANNY KONNIM, UNIT 311. THIRTY YEARS EARLIER.

No one at Saha was affected by the new respiratory infection circulating in Town. But toward the end of the pandemic, one pregnant woman who supposedly contracted it and was cured came to Saha with her hands around her very pregnant belly. The custodian asked if she was really cured, and Granny Konnim asked as well. The pregnant woman nodded at both of them.

"And the baby? The baby's fine?" asked Granny Konnim.

The woman nodded empathically. "The baby's fine. That's the problem."

This woman was very pregnant—so pregnant she couldn't walk or sit or stand comfortably—and no one at Saha could bring themselves to tell her to leave.

Heavy raindrops beat down on the windows as if trying to break in. The music from the radio was buried in the din of the rain. Granny Konnim turned off the radio, since she couldn't hear the music anyway, and her eyelids were growing heavy. Moments later, she heard a slow knock on her door and the faint voice of a woman.

"*Help* . . ."

More knocks on the door.

"*Hello . . . it's me. Please . . . help.*"

When Granny Konnim first came to Saha, she asked people to call her Granny even though she was far too young. So people awkwardly started calling her "Granny" and eventually got used to it. A few years had passed, and Granny Konnim was still young, but now she could be a "Granny." Yet this woman couldn't bring herself to call her that. Instead she simply said, "Hello."

Granny Konnim jumped up and ran to the door. Her hands were shaking so badly she fumbled with the latch. When she steadied her hands and opened the door, the woman collapsed on her. She had been crying so hard her face was awfully swollen. A few days earlier, Granny Konnim had seen the woman's belly hanging and thought she'd be due soon. The very same evening, she had checked on the delivery kit that was kept buried deep in her drawer. Sterilizing the umbilical cord scissors that had never been used, she had prayed she wouldn't have to open this kit in a rush in the middle of the night. Here she was, a few days later, opening the kit in the middle of a rainy night, hands shaking.

Lying on a pad creased from being spread open in a hurry, the woman was drenched in sweat and shaking as if she was about to die. In the dark room with the overhead fluorescents off, the dim incandescent bulb by the woman's head cast an orange light on her face. Rainwater streamed in a frenzy on the grimy surface of the windowpane, and sticky, slimy amniotic fluid and blood flowed out of the woman.

ON THE MAINLAND, Granny Konnim had been a midwife. Technically, she was a nurse's assistant at a small private clinic who ended up at a postnatal clinic through an old coworker's recommendation, whereupon she was referred to as "midwife" along with the rest of the staff. The clinic director was the only certified midwife.

The postnatal clinic was small, but it had steady business from women who felt ill at ease about the birthing procedure in hospitals. The clinic director did the deliveries. The other midwives' responsibility was to wrap the newborn in a clean towel and place it on the mother's chest, help the father cut the umbilical cord when the umbilical artery had stopped pulsing, throw out the placenta, blood, and other fluids, and clean up the delivery room. Watching the birthing process every day, Granny Konnim vowed never to give birth herself.

When Granny Konnim became the staff member who had worked at the clinic the longest, the director very cautiously suggested that Granny Konnim take on the procedures the director had been doing.

"It's illegal. No question about it, but . . . I just can't find a midwife who can handle the birthing process from start to finish. No one is qualified, experienced, or willing. You've seen so many, assisted so many, and we've done it all together."

Granny Konnim didn't like the sound of this. She wished she were a certified midwife, but that meant getting a nurse's license first. Which meant going to college. She didn't have the capacity, time, or money to study for the entrance exam, pass, and go to school for several years.

Seeing her hesitation, the director amended the conditions. "I'm not saying you'll be held fully responsible. I'll do most of the work, but when many women check in at the same time, could you help out just a little?"

Granny Konnim enrolled at a cram school for the midwife exam even though she wasn't qualified. She took the practice test and received scores that were a guaranteed pass. She felt confident she wasn't lacking in experience or in knowledge.

One night when two women were in labor at the same time, Granny Konnim did a delivery all by herself without the director's supervision. She had handled it quite capably. Nothing went wrong. Then a few months later she started handling procedures for *not* giving birth.

The clinic didn't divide the space very strictly according to procedures. The idea was to allow the women and their families to organically experience all the different parts of pregnancy and birth. In the lobby, a woman waiting for a checkup sat on the sofa and chatted with her family, while in another corner a woman in labor exercised on the birthing ball. In the recovery room equipped with cribs attached to every bed, new mothers recovered for about a week after birth, sharing the space with the women in high-risk pregnancies, those experiencing serious morning sickness, and other pregnancy-related pain.

In the exam room with a regular exam table—not a typical gynecologist's exam chair with stirrups—women received prenatal exams and gave birth. The exam table was used by women who wanted to give birth and those who did not.

The mainland allowed abortion under very few circumstances: if the biological parents had infectious or hereditary diseases, if the pregnancy was the result of rape, or if the pregnancy would cause health problems for the mother. Even in the early stages, the pregnant woman could not on her own choose to terminate. The penalty for unapproved abortion was severe. If caught, the woman would be punished with imprisonment or fines, and the person who performed the procedure would be punished with imprisonment. Medical professionals could have their licenses revoked.

Abortions were performed quietly at the clinic where Granny Konnim worked. It was the director's belief that life was to be cherished and every birth was a blessing, but that the decision to have or not to have a child was with the woman. Childbirth was in any case pain. It brought with it numerous kinds of aches and illnesses. The life of a woman that had been flowing according to cause and effect like a ribbon met an abrupt interruption with the birth of a child, as if cut with a blade. There was no telling how the child's life would turn out, either. A child coming into the world wasn't always the best thing.

The clinic director believed that the decision not to have a baby was equally as important as the decision to have a baby, and therefore the place where people came to have babies should also be the place people came to not have babies. Not everyone was well-informed or careful, and situations and minds could change. Above all, the director maintained that it was wrong to have a person's life fall to pieces because of a momentary lapse of judgment.

To those who were less than twelve weeks along, the clinic offered medication that controlled the hormones to terminate the pregnancy. To those who were less than six months along, the clinic performed the procedure without asking for any personal information. The cost was considerable, but not unreasonably so. The clinic worked in fear of being informed on or caught in a raid, and suffered from a deep sense of guilt instilled by society.

THE CLINIC WAS quiet on this day. The director had rushed off to assist a home delivery, and Granny Konnim was sitting on the exercise ball in the lobby. She leaned to the side, regained balance, leaned to the other side, and was righting herself again when the chime at the clinic door rang. No one was there. She must have heard wrong. So she didn't think much of it and now bounced on the ball out of boredom. The chime jingled again. Still no one at the door. What was going on? Granny Konnim got up and slowly approached the door, and the small silhouette on the other side of the glass whipped around and bolted. Granny Konnim took the trouble to put on her shoes, open the door, turn the corner, and make her way down the steps, where she found a young girl, definitely under twenty, sitting on the landing, a boy standing beside her.

"Are you the one who's been messing around?"

"I'm not messing around," the boy said with a rebellious look on his face.

"So then what do you want?"

The girl clenched her jaw, and the boy buried his face in his hands. Granny Konnim knew what they were there for, but waited for them to tell her.

A long while later, the girl asked, without meeting her eye, "I think I'm at about four months. Could I take meds for that?"

"You need the procedure done after twelve weeks."

"Okay . . . we're a little short on cash. Could you do the procedure now and we'll pay you back a little at a time?"

"No."

The girl seemed taken aback. She wasn't expecting to be turned down so harshly.

Granny Konnim took a firm stance, "Borrow, earn, steal, I don't care. Bring the procedure fee. You have to pay in advance."

She had no choice. The more desperate and dangerous the case, the stricter she had to be. She couldn't start giving handouts.

"And I think it's only fair that you take care of the bill," she said to the boy. "Do you understand what a big toll this will take on your young friend's body?"

The boy gave Granny Konnim a dirty look. "You go in," he said to the girl before running off.

Granny Konnim led the girl into the clinic. She felt uneasy making her wait in the lobby, so she opened an exam room for her and told her to make herself comfortable. The girl thanked her and jumped onto the exam table. Granny Konnim felt a jumble of something that wasn't relief, nervousness, or pity. Perhaps it was all three.

Scarcely half an hour later, the boy came in and put down a wad of cash on the counter. He must have looked up how much the procedure was; it was the fee exactly.

"Where'd you get the money so fast? This is no small amount for a kid like you."

"Stole it. You said steal."

"When does she want the procedure done? She'll be under sedation, but it's still anesthesia, and you want to be in pretty good physical condition for that. And no food after midnight before the procedure."

"Her physical condition won't get any better no matter what we do, and we haven't eaten a thing since yesterday, so how's that? Today's the only time we have. We would like it done now, please."

Granny Konnim thought for a moment and nodded. It was a simple procedure and it seemed like this was really the only chance these kids had.

"Fine. I'll prep and begin soon. But you have to be more careful from now on, okay?"

The girl was fast asleep on her stomach on the exam table. She couldn't bring herself to wake a girl so sound asleep that she didn't hear someone come in, so she watched her for a while. As the other midwife who came in to assist Granny Konnim sat the girl up and explained the procedure to her, the girl kept nodding off. When the IV needle went in her arm, she opened her eyes for a moment and said, "Mommy?" Then she closed her eyes again. Granny Konnim's heart went out to her.

Scraping off the clump of blood went swiftly and neatly. Granny Konnim covered the girl with a blanket and let her sleep off the sedative, but the girl didn't wake up. Shaking her didn't wake her up. Her pulse was growing weak, blood pressure and temperature were dropping. Granny Konnim was so panicked she couldn't do a thing. An illegal procedure by an unlicensed practician. *What's going to happen to me? And the clinic? And the director?* Her mind reeled. When she finally got it together and called the ambulance, the girl wasn't breathing. Granny Konnim fled from the mainland and ran all the way to the Saha Estates.

She had recurring nightmares of the girl suddenly opening her eyes and sitting up on the exam table. She woke up screaming every time. She calculated the amount of anesthesia again and pictured the face of the girl who would not open her eyes. Granny Konnim played the whole thing over and over in her head, from the moment she stuck the needle in the back of the girl's hand. It had gone exactly like all the procedures she had ever done. If it hadn't been illegal, would she have acted faster in the emergency situation? Would the girl have received the procedure in a safer environment? Even the regrets sounded like excuses and tormented her.

Granny Konnim knew that it was all her fault. She'd made such a huge mistake and wasn't penalized for it; she did not take responsibility. She lived each day thinking she would have to pay one day, or else she would end up punishing herself.

GRANNY KONNIM LOOKED into the crying woman's eyes.

"If you cry or scream, you'll tire yourself out," she said. "You won't have strength left when it's time to push. So stop crying. Don't waste your energy. When I say push, push like you're taking a dump. It'll be over before you know it."

The woman stopped crying. Taking a deep breath in, holding it, and slowly breathing out at Granny Konnim's direction, the woman must have had some sort of premonition, for she suddenly grabbed Granny Konnim's hand and implored her not to give the baby away to anyone—and raise the child herself.

The baby crowned. It was black. Too black. Granny Konnim was alarmed but tried to keep calm. When she told the mother she could see the head, the woman let out a deep, long groan. The head popped out, ripped the perineum in all directions, and the narrower shoulders and body slid out through the path the head had cleared.

The baby had its eyes closed with its arms crossed over its chest. Its long, thick hair clung to its face and covered its eyes. When she inserted the suction device in the baby's mouth to remove fluids, she felt something hard. She cautiously lifted the baby's lips. Four on top, four on the bottom, eight teeth altogether. A chill ran up from her tailbone to the top of her head, and her arms went so weak she almost dropped the baby. A fear she'd never experienced in all the years she'd been delivering babies came over her.

Baby with eyes closed but making a curious face as if pretending to sleep, mother with eyes closed forever after expelling the baby and all she had. The face of the girl from long ago overlapped with the face of the mother who lay with her mouth open as if she had something left to say. Granny Konnim vowed to herself that she would keep her promise to the mother no matter what.

The rain stopped the instant the baby was born, the night grew ever deeper, and Granny Konnim, overcome with drowsiness as if enchanted by the darkness, wrapped the baby in a towel and held it in her arms as she nodded off on the floor. The baby shuddered and then shuddered again moments later. When she carefully pulled the towel down below the baby's chin, the baby frowned at her, looked around, and hiccupped. The baby looked toward the window and back at her. Its eyes were focused and sharp.

The research center took the mother's body. While the people from the research center packed her up, a purring that could only come from an animal kept rattling from the bundle of blanket Granny Konnim was holding. A man reached for the bundle, faint smile lines starting to form around his mouth.

Granny Konnim jumped back in horror. The man raised his hands, showing his palms, and tried to smile warmly.

"You can't raise it on your own," he said, slowly moving back toward her. "We just want to see if we might be of help."

As scared of the baby as she was suspicious of the man, she couldn't spurn this shady generosity. While she was trying to think of what to do, the man pulled the blanket back with his right index finger. His eyebrows rose and fell. His expression was unchanged, but what he saw left him breathless.

"You can't raise it on your own. Call us anytime. We'll do the best we can." He left her a card with no name or address, just an office number.

At the end of an exceptionally dry autumn, on a night that brought torrential downpour and thunder, Woomi was born and her mother died. Exactly two weeks from the day Woomi's mother came to the Saha Estates.

From that night on, the Saha residents began giving birth with Granny Konnim's help. As children were brought into the world and raised on the Estates, the place became a world unto itself.

GRANNY KONNIM FED Woomi barley tea with a spoon for several days following her birth, and when it became clear that Granny Konnim would be raising Woomi, she bought infant formula at the supermarket. *She's never been breastfed. Would she know how to use a bottle?* Granny Konnim thought with a heavy heart as she held Woomi in her left arm and the bottle in her right. She gently touched Woomi's left cheek with the rubber nipple smelling of sweet formula. Woomi threw her head to the left and drank the formula, sucking on the rubber nipple so hard she tore it off.

Woomi emptied the bottle in no time and continued to suck at the air. Granny Konnim held her up. Woomi let out a long burp, like an adult, and immediately overflowed the diaper Granny Konnim had fashioned out of an old blanket. From that moment on, Woomi cried so hard her face turned from red to black, stopping only when Granny Konnim gave her the formula, which she drank fervently and immediately shot out the other end. Granny Konnim had to call the number on the card.

She asked for help matter-of-factly so as to come off entitled. She thought she had to do that much to keep her promise to Woomi's mother. She hid her fears and spoke nonchalantly.

"I don't care if the kid lives or dies," she said. "But I don't want to give it away. Just don't want to."

Granny Konnim agreed to let the research center examine and record Woomi's development in exchange for providing medical treatment and helping her grow. From that day on, Woomi consumed a special formula the research center provided. She received treatment at the research center when she was hurt or sick. As a child visiting the research center with a nervous Granny Konnim, Woomi did not know that she was the recipient of benefits beyond a mere Saha's wild imaginings. And so she did not understand the strange hostility directed at her by the ailing, irritable adults at Saha. It made her self-conscious without knowing why, and sometimes even angry.

Woomi felt the same way at the research center. The waiting room staff recognized Woomi and Granny Konnim and were friendly when they asked after them, but never let them into the research center right away. They called the office, spoke with the person in charge, checked their fingerprints, and then led them to the elevators. The elevator button could not be pressed without the staff's key card, and once they were inside it only opened on the floor the staff selected. They saw different research staff each time, whose name tags were always removed from their lab coats. Woomi and Granny Konnim were kept at a friendly, polite arm's length.

The research center's summons were irregular, sometimes once or twice a year, other times weekly.

"Please undress her," said the male researcher with a youngish face as he looked into the monitor. Woomi was twelve then, standing with her shoulders rolled in, and Granny Konnim took her time undoing her buttons. She asked, "Just the blouse?"

"Top, bottom, underwear, all of it, please."

"Isn't this a bit rude? She's all grown up," Granny Konnim remarked.

The researcher replied with a friendly smile, "No one goes into surgery and gets shots fully dressed at a hospital. Think of this place as a hospital. Well, it is a hospital to our young friend here."

Woomi mumbled quietly to herself, "I'm not your friend, guy." The researchers were frequently shocked and often concerned about what they found as they examined Woomi, but they never fully explained anything to Granny Konnim. They said they didn't know what was going on. They were new recruits who were just following orders and reporting to their superiors—diagnoses, decisions, prognoses were all up to the person in charge, they said, as if they were all given the same prompt to memorize in case Granny Konnim asked. They didn't tell her who the person in charge was, either. All Granny Konnim could do was go along with their requests. The fear, doubt, and despair Granny Konnim felt when that happened was passed on wholly to Woomi as well.

THE MAN CAME to Saha roughly ten years ago, when Woomi was twenty. He wouldn't say where he'd been and what he'd done, or why he had to hide out in the Saha Estates. Saha residents were wary of this man, who was so brazen despite his mysterious past, but Granny Konnim was not.

"Most people who can't tell you about their past aren't bad," she defended him. "It's the ones that lie about it that are bad."

Soon after the man's arrival, the original custodian of Saha Estates became gravely ill and the man took over his position. This happened, once again, by Granny Konnim's recommendation. Besides, there were no other options. Saha residents referred to the new custodian as "old man."

The old man, unfamiliar as he was with the uniqueness of the Saha Estates and the people who lived there, was barely managing to keep the minor and major problems under control. Then a baby suddenly fell in his lap. The baby, which looked no more than a hundred days old, was wrapped tightly in a blanket and left at the custodian's office door without so much as a note. The blanket and onesie looked expensive at a glance, and the baby had the lovely scent of milk. It kept moving its plump lips as if it were feeding in its dream, and a thin, long trace of spit-up extended from the corner of its mouth.

The old man didn't know what to do. He carried the baby exactly as he found it, went all the way up to Granny Konnim's door, then came back to his office, put down the bundle, went back to Granny Konnim's, glanced into the window where the light was on, and came back to his office again. A man from Building A who was watching all of this in the yard as he smoked sauntered into the custodian's office and asked, "Hey, are you sweet on Granny Konnim?"

"Shut up, you lunatic."

"Well, you do that thing whenever Granny Konnim's around. You get antsy and you stammer and excuse yourself. You're not like that with any of the rest of us. You're rude to all of us, but so careful around Granny Konnim. Gee, I wonder why. If you don't have a thing for her, maybe she knows your secret?"

The old man pulled back the cover on the bundle just enough to show him. The man quickly tossed his cigarette far away and waved the smoke away with both arms.

"I don't know if there's anyone besides Granny Konnim who would take it," said the man from Building A.

"She had such a hard time raising Woomi all on her own . . . I couldn't bring myself to ask," said the old man.

"Is Woomi your kid? Why are you sorry she had a hard time with Woomi? You're acting real suspicious."

The man craned his neck to take another look at the baby. "Cute kid," he said, and sauntered out of the office without another word.

In the end, the old man brought the baby to Granny Konnim's. She tapped the baby's cheek, and the baby's head followed her finger. He sucked at the air with his tongue resting on the lower lip.

"You're hungry, aren't you?"

Granny Konnim held the baby close to her chest, turned her head, and breathed out, letting the air through her nose a little at a time. The old man realized that she was trying not to let the baby see that she was sighing, and took it as a sign that she would take it. He was relieved.

IN TOWN, BABIES aren't thrown away. Town values human life above all else, so anyone, even a Saha, can receive medical treatment throughout their pregnancy and deliver safely, no questions asked, for free. Just up until the birth of the child. So there are no incidents of young schoolgirls having babies alone in a bathroom. However, only the properly insured get to be discharged from the hospital with the baby without extra cost. The mothers who were uninsured or couldn't reveal their identities ran away, leaving their babies at the hospital. The babies were sent to the orphanage, where they received nutrition, care, adequate medical and educational support, and left the home with L2 status at seventeen.

In Town, where workers of only the highest quality were granted citizenship, productivity and GDP were staggeringly high but menial labor forces were in short supply. Where there were people who ate, slept, and produced waste, there had to be people to make the food, clean the homes, and dispose of the waste. For companies, factories, and research centers to function, someone had to take care of mindless work. But Town Citizens didn't want to take on such work. With a population so small, the market for such work was also bound to be small.

This was why Town issued temporary L2 status to those who didn't qualify for citizenship. The state even turned a blind eye to the illegal residents who didn't qualify. The L2 and Saha population thus grew over the years and, roughly a decade after the founding of Town, reached thirty percent of the population. This was no small proportion. It was a demographic large enough to effect change, but there was no significant mobilizing for decades.

Initially, memories of the Butterfly Riot roughly thirty years ago held them back. The images of helitankers dropping water on the protesters, and soldiers and police forces overwhelming civilian protesters in numbers and with weapons, lingered. Those who took part in the riot were killed, maimed, or arrested. Every last one of them was caught in the end—at a dead-end street, a rooftop, a bathroom stall, or under the wall of some stranger's roof, if not that very day, the following day, the following month, and even the following year. Speaking, writing, even drawing about the things that happened on that day were considered proof of participation and were punishable by law. No one dared speak of the Butterfly Riot. Undocumented and undiscussed, the incident was distorted in people's memories and became fuel for fear.

By the time memories of the Butterfly Riot had more or less faded, the children and grandchildren of the original Town L2s had largely replaced them and become the new

L2 population. There was no sense of rebellion or doubt in the children who were born L2s. *Innateness* or *duty* weren't the right words; *destiny* was too grand. Life was what it was. They made money doing what they were assigned to do, did not wonder about how the kids they grew up with turned out, renewed their L2 status every two years, met someone similar, fell in love, had a child, and left it at the hospital.

The child that ended up in Granny Konnim's arms was different from the babies that were left at the hospital. It was raised in an unstable environment where it was not adequately provided for. As a Saha, not even an L2, he grew up harboring a question that would never be answered and an anger directed at no one in particular. An "abandoned child," one of his kind in the Saha Estates and perhaps all of Town. The old man referred to the baby as the "motherless kid." Woomi hated hearing that and told him so. He didn't see what the problem was.

"Some people don't have fathers, you see," he said. "There is no such thing as a child that never had a mother to begin with. She either dies, abandons the child, has the baby taken away, something like that. Do you know why the kids who grow up in the orphanage and become L2s get pregnant and leave their children at the hospitals, and then make more L2s like it's nothing? It's because they think they don't even know what mothers are. They think they never had one to begin with. That such a thing is possible. I'm not trying to say this kid *never* had a mother. I'm actually trying to remind him that he did have a mother at one point."

Woomi thought for a moment about her own mother. The

old man, Granny Konnim—everyone at the Saha Estates must have had a mother, she realized.

"Who do you think the kid's mother is?"

"Don't know. But she's better than the parents who leave their babies at the hospital."

"Seeing as she left the baby here, she probably didn't have the baby at a hospital. Where could she possibly have had him?"

"Maybe there's another place like the Saha Estates out there."

Woomi was baffled by the old man's ludicrous conjecture.

"What, you think this is the only one of its kind?" the old man said, smiling bitterly at Woomi, who was at a loss for words. "Think of all the cycles of hell. Fire hell, water hell, ice hell, needle hell; somewhere down that avenue is the Saha Estates, and next to that is the neighboring hell where that kid was born."

Born in hell and raised in another hell. Woomi was scared and sorry for the baby, now Granny Konnim's charge and Woomi's younger brother.

THE BABY'S DEVELOPMENT was slow-going. Another baby, who was born around the same time downstairs, was lifting its head up, turning over, and pushing itself forward using its arms, but the baby at Woomi's lay still, looking up at the ceiling.

"Granny, do you think something's wrong with him? Maybe the parents knew and threw him out."

"He eats, poops, plays, and sleeps well at night. I think he's very healthy," said Granny Konnim.

While Granny Konnim was out, Woomi tried sitting the baby up, supporting his head and pointing out which muscles to engage. She lay next to him and showed him how to roll over. The baby waved his arms and legs in the air with no intention of following her. By the time the baby downstairs was crawling pretty fast, the boy started turning over with much effort, banging his heavy head. Face on the floor, the boy cried out of frustration. Woomi would begrudge the slow-developing baby and leave it to cry; Granny Konnim would come over and lay the baby on his back. The baby continued to be docile, and the back of his head was flat.

IT WAS EARLY EVENING. The baby had gone to sleep early with his mouth open and his arms over his head. Woomi and Granny Konnim did not have to lower their voices or be quiet with the dishes and silverware, as the baby slept through the noise without so much as a stir.

"Doesn't he hear us? How does he sleep through everything?"

"He's a perfect lamb, that's why. You weren't like that."

"What was I like?"

"You didn't sleep unless I held you. When I put you down, you would kick and scream. And boy, were you heavy. I aged ten years because of you. You'd better carry me around on your back when I'm old and infirm."

Granny Konnim's story gave Woomi a great idea.

"Maybe he's like that because we don't hold him enough. Maybe that's why he can hardly hold his head up."

"I suppose babies learn to use their muscles faster if you hold them up more and change their positions. They'll hold themselves up better. But what's the big deal if you learn to pick your head up or move or walk a month or two later than everyone else? How's that important?"

Woomi was immersed in thought for a while as she watched the baby sleep.

"It's important to me, Granny," she began. "It's upsetting that our baby is slower than the baby downstairs. I don't like how the guy downstairs asks me why our baby is lying around all day. He's pretending to be worried about our baby, but he's really just showing off. Some things are pleasant, and other things are upsetting. I am *upset* that our baby is slow. How can you say that these feelings are not important?"

The following day, Woomi started holding the baby every chance she got. She was clumsy and awkward, and she was conscious of the neighbors' eyes, but she did her best. She brought the baby out to where Granny Konnim was working in the garden, walked around the playground, and hung around with the children playing in the yard. The baby stretched his legs, held his head up, and waved his arms. The baby, who had been tame as a lamb, started to fuss now that Woomi was picking him up. Night and day, the baby fussed and refused to sleep. He rolled all around the apartment, and, once he started crawling, knocked over glasses of water, tore pages out of books, and got himself into trouble. Woomi found it exhausting to watch the baby. Granny Konnim advised her to just let the baby cry it out when she was tired.

"A good cry will make his voice stronger."

"Granny, did you let me cry it out, too?"

"I didn't have to. You were crying all the time anyway."

Woomi held the crying baby, comforted him, cleaned up his mess, and all of a sudden realized he didn't have a name. It had been three months since he'd arrived at the Saha Estates, and Granny Konnim and Woomi had always referred to the baby as "our little lamb." There was no reason to call the baby by a name when he never cried, fussed, or made trouble. Woomi decided to name him. She took one syllable from her own name and another from Granny Konnim's and named him Woonim.

"Yech, no!" Granny Konnim was horrified. "Leave my name out of this!"

So Woomi changed it to Wooyon—*chance*. Granny Konnim gently tried it on the baby, "Wooyon, honey. It's nice." So the baby had a name.

Babies fuss when there's someone around to care and watch over them. If they fuss, someone picks them up and calls them by their name. This leads to more fussing and more being held, and growing. For some time, Wooyon called both Woomi and Granny Konnim "mama." Woomi just figured "nuna"—*older sister*—was harder to pronounce than "mama," and didn't think much of it, but Granny Konnim was horrified once again.

"Don't call me your mama, I'm not your mama! Say 'granny.' GRA-nny."

Wooyon skipped "gram," "gwam," and "gammy," and said "granny" flawlessly on his first try. Woomi was shocked, and so was Granny Konnim, who'd instructed him to say it. It was a long time, however, before he could say other things besides "mama" and "granny." Wooyon learned to walk, talk, and even go potty later than the baby downstairs.

A YOUNG COUPLE lived in Building B, Unit 316. The husband and wife both seemed normal enough, but at one point they stopped going to work, stayed in the house all day, and only went out together occasionally. The woman wore long sleeves and masks in the middle of summer, which wasn't very common but not altogether strange. Nevertheless, it sparked rumors. *The husband is very jealous. The wife is sick. The couple has joined a cult.*

One early morning, the wife came out by herself to take out the trash. She threw two bulging black plastic bags containing who knew what in the designated bins, and walked over to the vegetable garden. After a warm winter in which it rained more than it snowed, Granny Konnim's garden was sprouting green shoots that were too tiny to identify. The woman stood at the garden, closed her eyes, and swung her arms open and gathered them back as she took deep breaths. The front of her fluffy ivory sweater, which came down over her knees, parted and revealed a baby bump.

When she ran into the woman, Granny Konnim felt her stomach to confirm the baby was kicking, but never examined her in earnest. The couple didn't want an exam. They said they would handle the delivery on their own. Woomi was worried about the man—who'd probably never even held a baby—delivering a child. Granny Konnim, on the other hand, said that's how they all did it in the past and there was no reason to fuss. Woomi thought Granny Konnim was just saying that because she'd never given birth herself, but she didn't press her. The woman's stomach was growing daily, and Woomi's fears were growing just as much as the woman's belly.

"Granny, did you see the woman in 316? Her stomach is too big. Do you think it's twins?"

Granny Konnim didn't reply.

ONE LATE NIGHT, the couple came to see Granny Konnim. They said the baby was on the larger side and the mother wasn't in good health, and that they'd managed after much effort to find a place to deliver the child safely, so they wanted to say goodbye. Granny Konnim found it strange that the couple had dropped by her place to say goodbye and that there was a place where people from the Saha Estates could have a baby and bring it home, but all she could do was wish them luck.

The woman, who was in a kneeling position, shifted uncomfortably and stroked her belly. The man reached a trembling hand to hold hers, and she placed her other hand on top of his. Doubt, fear, and sadness alighted one on top of the other on the stomach ready to rip apart. Frightened like someone who'd placed another rock on top a precariously stacked tower of rocks, Granny Konnim repeated, to get the couple to leave, "Get to bed early tonight. Good luck and safe travels."

The couple did not answer or get up.

"Granny Konnim," the man started with difficulty after a long pause. "We wanted to ask you . . ."

Another long pause ensued.

"Did you have something you wanted to say?" Granny Konnim asked.

Tears fell from the woman's eyes, and the man hung his head.

"We'd like you to examine her."

Granny Konnim's blanket with small, colorful flowers was quite faded, with lint scattered like pollen. Lying back on the blanket, breathing in the sour old-lady smell, the woman was oddly very comforted. Sleep came over her.

Granny Konnim ran her hands over the woman's stomach, its skin stretched so tautly that the veins were clearly visible, and felt around to examine the baby underneath. *Oh*. The size of the head, the movement of the arms and legs, and even the baby's position were unlike anything Granny Konnim had encountered before. But the baby was already big and it seemed getting it out quickly was the answer. Granny Konnim said the only thing she could say to them: "Good luck and safe travels."

Neither came to pass. A week later, the man came back dragging an empty suitcase behind him like fate and said both child and mother died. No one asked him a thing. The man went into seclusion again in his apartment, this time alone.

HEAVY RAINS DUG up the earth in the garden. The shallow roots were exposed and the fruit that fell prematurely sat in puddles. Granny Konnim came out early in her raincoat with a hole in the underarm to cover the exposed roots, pack down the earth where she could, and support the stalks with wooden sticks. Gathering the fruit that was salvageable, she muttered, "Shame, such a shame."

Drenched and shivering in her raincoat, she was coming out of the garden with a handful of still-green cherry tomatoes when she spotted a shadow on the third-floor walkway of Building B. The man from 316 was looking down at the garden. There was significant distance between them and she couldn't see his face well, but she knew that they were regarding each other.

Granny Konnim pushed the air toward him with the back of her hand, gesturing at him to go back inside. He stood still, his gaze fixed on her. She gestured at him again. Standing in the garden as rain kept falling, she gestured at him again and again to go inside. After a long while, the man bowed to her, bending deep at the waist, and went into 316. Granny Konnim came down with a terrible flu.

WOOMI, UNIT 311

The research center had thousands of staff, and thousands from the affiliated university, high school, and gift program used the various facilities and labs—and yet the place always seemed deserted to Woomi. People walking at a slow pace, speaking softly, scarcely making eye contact. On days when she did not run into a single person in the waiting room, the hall, or elevator, the quiet came across as oppressive.

Recording height and weight, blood pressure, EEG, drawing blood . . . At the end of the row of exam booths, which were divided with transparent panels, there was a waiting space with an armchair and a coffee table, and on the coffee table always the same brand of five-hundred-milliliter bottled water. When she first started coming here, Woomi did not even touch the water. Now she emptied the bottle in one gulp.

The female researcher with her lab coat sleeve rolled up

had cold, damp fingertips. Woomi stared numbly at the deft hands of the woman taking a disposable syringe out of the wrapper. She had pretty fingernails. She also had a bright face, gentle eyes, and long fingers, but Woomi envied her fingernails, of all things—the gentle curve of the surface, solid, clean. An even pink all over. She hadn't tidied her cuticles, nor did she wear nail polish, but the fingernails revealed that they belonged to a very neat person.

The woman rubbed an alcohol-soaked cotton ball on Woomi's arm. The chill of evaporating alcohol instantly spread all over her body. Woomi was suddenly brought back to reality, as if waking with a start. The woman hummed a tune as she picked up the syringe from the tray, and Woomi quickly turned her head and shut her eyes tight. She tried to relax her arm, but she couldn't. More than the stab of the needle, pain of the needle breaking skin and entering, the tension in her arm was harder to stand.

"All done," the woman said, laughing softly. "Cute. Closed eyes and everything."

Cute. Said as if to herself. The woman never called Woomi by her name, and Woomi didn't know the woman's name. Not once did the same person examine Woomi. She had felt frustrated, vulnerable, and angry about this, but at some point began to think that was a good thing. She'd once asked what the injection was for. She must have been around ten. The male researcher answered in a reassuring tone, "It's to make you feel better."

"But I'm not sick."

The man had raised an eyebrow at Woomi's reply, rolled

his eyes, and came up with the answer, "You'll be able to make other people feel better." Young Woomi didn't fully understand what he meant. So she said very clearly once more, "I. Am. Fine." The man only laughed.

Woomi asked the female researcher with the healthy fingernails, "What's the shot for?"

The woman only smiled. Woomi came out of the exam room pressing a cotton pad to the injection site and walked down the hall with the woman. The floor, walls, and ceiling were all the same suffocating gray. They passed a succession of rectangular windows all with identical venetian blinds; at the end of the hall was a picture that took up half the wall. A baby. Chubby cheeks and chin bursting with baby fat, eyes keen and enormous, staring out like the eyes of an adult. The picture wasn't a good fit for the research center, but the end of a long hall was the perfect place for it. Woomi had always taken in this picture with great interest.

Walking with her eyes locked on the baby's, Woomi stopped when she felt the floor and ceiling stretch like taffy and get sucked into a tightening spiral at the far end of the hall.

The click of the woman's heels stopped as well. "What's wrong?"

The whirl rushed at Woomi from the end of the hall, and the baby's eyes, profound and gigantic, were right before Woomi's nose. Her consciousness sank and faded like effervescing soda bubbles. A cold hand tapped Woomi on the face twice: *Tap, tap*. Even as Woomi was fading, she thought of the cold hand, the fingers that grazed her arm, and the pink fingernails. The thud of footsteps rushed toward her heart.

Unfazed voices. *Do you think it was the booster shot? It can't be working already. BP is low.* Woomi's body floated up. *Could this be a dream?*

GREEN AS FAR as the eye could see. Woomi lay in the shade of a tree. Strong branches reaching out in all directions, their leaves lush with dew, ready to fall at the gentlest touch. The leaves fluttered wildly. Sunlight so strong Woomi could hardly look at it filtering down through the leaves. Suddenly she realized she couldn't feel the earth beneath her, nor the leaves and the breeze. Only then did the window come into view. Trees, leaves, and sun on the other side of the window. All these living things were a tableau, and Woomi thought perhaps she, too, was a still life in a great frame.

The door opened and the same researcher from before entered. Woomi slowly sat up and looked around the room. Next to the cot where she sat were a round tea table, two metal chairs, one overhead light built into the ceiling, and a security camera in one corner. She must have been watching Woomi through that camera.

Putting down a mug on the tea table, the woman said to Woomi, "Your blood pressure is a little low. I think you got dizzy all of a sudden. Have some warm tea and you'll feel better."

Woomi had fought not to let go of her hearing, as all other senses were fading: *Booster shot.* It could be the booster shot. Woomi picked up the mug with both hands and slurped. Bitter, fresh taste of herb. The woman watched as Woomi put down the mug and took a deep breath.

"You might get a headache or flu-like symptoms," she said, handing her a packet of medication. "Don't take just any painkiller. This will help. Come back tomorrow for the same shot and then Monday at nine a.m. for a blood draw."

"Okay."

That was all Woomi could say in that moment.

WOOMI HAD NEVER given much thought to her gender or identity. She had no complaints about how she looked and had no desire to be pretty. But as she grew tall and her pelvis and breasts developed, she did not menstruate.

In her seventeenth summer, she was waiting fearfully for her first period. On her way back from the research center one day, Woomi bought herself a barrette at a stall near a girls' school. A simple purple ribbon with no patterns. When she said she'd like it gift-wrapped, the vendor smiled and said he didn't have any tissue paper. Woomi put the pin deep inside her bag.

She went into an empty bathroom in a commercial building and put the barrette in her hair. It looked better than she had expected. She was looking back and forth between her face and the barrette when the bathroom door swung open. Woomi snatched the barrette off her head. The pin snapped in two in her enormous grasp. And at the same time, something spilled out from between her legs. *Oh.* Clutching the front of her T-shirt lest her thumping heart break out of her ribs, tear through her flesh, and jump out, Woomi dashed into a stall and pulled her pants down. Her underwear and pants were soaked with urine. She'd had a dumb accident, but she was calm. Except, an emotion had slipped right out.

Woomi's period started three months later, and she was unmoved by it. Both cycle and flow were irregular and the cramps were horrific. It was so unbearable it felt like an illness, not a part of growing up. Her ob-gyn checkups began. She had a small lump on her ovaries that they recommended she have removed by undergoing a procedure that required general anesthesia, so she accepted. Several times, she was told only after the fact that a simple procedure was done on her. She was receiving regular treatments for endometriosis. Lights so bright they stung her eyes, stirrups that kept her legs spread wide apart, researchers conversing with their faces up in between her legs, gesturing and talking among themselves. Woomi gritted her teeth and thought of the things she had to endure to survive.

ON MONDAY MORNING, Woomi arrived at the research center much earlier than her appointment. She had a terrible headache, possibly from being tense. When she asked if it would be okay to get her blood drawn in this state, the researcher—again, someone she had never seen before—smiled and said it would be fine.

"I'm sorry you have a headache. I guess it's side effects from the booster shot. Many people complained of backaches. Did you sleep okay? It's been uncomfortable, huh?"

There was sincere concern in his voice. Woomi's headache was alleviated as she felt less anxious. Looking at the misshapen nose of the researcher tapping the crook of her arm to find her vein, she thought about the things he let slip. *Side effects from the booster shot . . . Many people complained of backaches* . . . So what Woomi was injected with was definitely a booster shot, and there were others who received the same booster shot. Did he really let these things slip without an agenda?

Woomi leaned back in the bed, which was set at about a forty-degree angle, with IV lines in both arms.

"This will take about two hours. Call me if you need anything."

The man left with simple instructions. The maroon blood that came out of Woomi's left arm flowed into a blood component separator that was an elaborate block of buttons, wires, and tubes. Then the blood reentered through the line on the back of Woomi's right hand.

It was hard to move. Woomi closed her eyes, but the lighting was too bright and the whir of the machine too loud. How about some music? Woomi thought about calling for the man, but then thought better of it. She clenched and opened her fists when her arms tingled. That seemed to relieve the symptoms. The process took longer than she expected and Woomi wound up trapped in the bed for a little over three hours, but couldn't fall asleep. Her head still hurt and her body felt stiff by the time she was done, but worst of all, she badly needed to go to the bathroom.

As Woomi made her way to the elevator, the same male researcher followed her, slowly closing the distance between them. *If he keeps getting closer at this rate,* Woomi thought, *we could be holding hands by the time we reach the end of the hall.* He kept making small talk. Woomi gave quick, curt responses to his questions and waited for an opportunity to get away. Did you take the bus here? Yes. It was exhausting at the lab today, huh? A little. You did well. What did you take today? White blood cells.

Such conversations sometimes took place in code between Woomi and the researchers. She met someone different each time, and never the same person twice, but the conversations went more or less the same way. A string of questions and answers were passed back and forth until the moment came when the roles flipped in the blink of an eye. Most research- ers didn't understand Woomi's questions and asked her what she meant, but some were able to continue the conversation. Through her short exchanges with them, she was able to piece together over the years that she was providing the lab with her blood, stem cells, white blood cells, and eggs. Why did they need all this and how was it used, Woomi had no idea. There were never enough pieces to complete the puzzle. The lack of information keeping her in the dark was not as unbearable as the wild conjectures in her head exacerbating her anxiety.

Did the researchers even know each other? There was a time when Woomi believed there was an organization within the research center that shared a set of agreements and rules. But the clues she gathered and the areas they examined were too random, sometimes even overlapped, and some informa- tion was hard to trust. She believed the ones who provided her with information were just individual reprobates, per- haps a large, loosely connected group that shared this "misfit" behavior.

The man tapped his security card on the touch panel by the elevator door, and punched in "4" when the screen lit up.

"You must have had a checkup at the ob-gyn last time. You

need to have a biopsy, so you'll be heading down to the exam room on the fourth floor. When you get to the fourth floor, the exam room technician will meet you by the elevator."

Hands deep in her pockets, Woomi stood one step behind the man and waited for the elevator. There was a bun wrapper crumpled up in her pocket that she couldn't remember shoving there. She thought of the story of Hansel and Gretel. Hansel ripped little pieces of his bread to make a trail that would lead him home. Woomi felt she was the bread that was ripped and thrown on the ground to serve as signposts. *If they keep ripping out pieces of me, what will be left?* The birds pecked at Hansel's bread until there was nothing, and Hansel and Gretel could not find their way home.

Sara's cold face came to mind. Sara's voice was firm even as she was crying: *I want a proper life. Not to be merely alive, but to really live.* To really live. Perhaps Woomi's confusion and inquiries also came from the impulse to really live.

"What if I don't want to get the biopsy?" Woomi asked abruptly.

"Pardon?" The man turned and gave her a puzzled look.

"I don't want the biopsy. I'm going home."

Woomi had never voiced her opinion at the research center before. She didn't think it was something that could be done. Each time the research center summoned her, she came, followed instructions, was examined, received shots, and took medication. Granny Konnim always told Woomi, "You're not healthy." Woomi didn't have pains or discomforts anywhere, but took it for granted that she was not a healthy person. To Woomi, an illness wasn't a diagnosis based on symptoms and signs. It was a fate one was born with. Feeling pain and discomfort was not necessarily a sign of poor health, but it was poor health that required exams and treatments—the causal relationship only existed in the latter.

When someone has spent her entire life thinking, *Life is what it is*, it takes time for her to see that "what it is" does not *have* to be her life. Woomi needed time. The elevator arrived, and Woomi did not get in.

"Please press first floor. I'm going home."

"I was given instructions to send you to the exam room on the fourth floor when you're done with the blood collection, and I don't have a say."

"Send me to the first floor."

"I can't just say, *Okay, then, have a safe trip home*. But I could ask permission. You'll have to wait a bit. Alternatively, you could run away. I'm not a good runner."

Woomi wondered for a moment if the man was joking. Then she grabbed the man's shoulders, using him as a springboard, flew up in the air to break the security camera in the middle of the ceiling, and kicked the man in the stomach while she was at it. The man gasped, let out a sharp groan that Woomi couldn't tell was an inhale or exhale, and doubled over. Woomi was about to snatch the security card hanging from his neck when she heard footsteps coming from the nearby stairwell. Already? Woomi ran to the first door she could reach. The knob turned and the door opened. There was no time for second-guessing. She ducked in.

IT WAS A conference room. The lights were off, and around the large circular conference table were a dozen chairs. On the screen opposite the door was a chart and numbers she couldn't make sense of, and a middle-age man was standing next to the screen shooting a laser into the air with a pointer. His expression was calm, as if he knew Woomi would be dropping by.

"There's space behind the screen," he said.

At the click of the remote control, the screen rolled up. Shouts, sirens, footsteps echoed down the hall. Woomi hid and the man rolled down the screen again. Was this man another "reprobate"? Woomi heard a knock on the door, followed immediately by the latch clicking, and walkie-talkie static. She shut her eyes tight. The static came toward her and receded. Woomi covered her ears as best she could, but the shrill voice of a woman squeezed its way in.

"Are you alone?"

"I'm prepping for a meeting," said the man. "There's a meeting here in twenty minutes. It's a meeting that requires level-one clearance. The director and the chairperson will be in attendance. I still have some work left to do. Do you mind if I keep working?"

As the walkie-talkie sound receded further, the man said, "I heard a commotion outside. Is something wrong?"

"A Master Key assaulted a researcher and ran away," the voice said. "I doubt it got very far."

Master Key? Is that what I am? She'd never been referenced by name or by number at the research center. Woomi felt an odd sense of betrayal to know that she'd been referred to by such a strange term all this time.

"Excuse me," the voice said, and went out the door. Long after the sound of the walkie-talkie had left, the man still had not given Woomi the all-clear. Woomi waited.

The man spoke to Woomi with the screen still between

them. "Take the stairs to the basement. And leave by the parking lot entrance. You need an access key to get into the stairwell. You can take mine. You'll be safe once you're out of the building. At least for now."

The screen went up, and the man handed her the key card that had been hanging from his neck.

"What's a Master Key?" Woomi asked, taking the card.

"Think of it as one of the projects at the lab. I don't really know, either, apart from the fact that you are helping research vaccines and incurable diseases."

"Why me?"

"You're a survivor."

"We're all alive."

"You survived a situation that was difficult to survive," he said. "They probably want to know why. And they need you."

Woomi did not notice that she was clenching and slowly bending the card in her hand.

The man grabbed Woomi firmly by the wrist. "Run."

"No, I must find out what's happening to me."

"And how will you do that?"

Woomi couldn't answer.

"Just go back for now," he said. "I'll help you. There are people willing to help."

"Why . . . should I believe you?"

The man gazed at Woomi. "I've been waiting. I want to help."

Inside Woomi's heart was a beast raised on rage. It was trained to be vicious—to sink its fangs in the enemy's throat and make the kill. The claws grew sharp and its temperament was so hostile she could hardly keep it locked up. It sometimes scratched Woomi from the inside. But now the beast was lying down on all fours, belly on the ground. Woomi saw that the beast wasn't raised on rage, but on loneliness.

THE RED LIGHT blinked on the security camera over the side door. Someone was watching from some unseen place. Woomi stood with her back against the door and tapped the man's security card on the sensor. Click. The sound of a bolt unlocking, a closed door opening, a sinister welcome.

As promised, the man called Woomi on the following evening. On Thursday night between 11:25 and 11:30 she was to enter the research complex through the back gate that was guarded by an unmanned automated security system, come up over the hill, through the parking lot, and into the main building.

"Someone from the security team will look out for you. So you must come between eleven twenty-five and eleven-thirty. Not a second sooner or later."

Woomi held the phone receiver in one hand and the man's security card in the other. "But if I come in through the back gate and the basement door, wouldn't it leave a record?"

"It doesn't matter."

It doesn't matter. Not *It's okay,* or *It won't be a problem,* but *It doesn't matter.* The man's indifferent words weighed heavy on Woomi.

Checkups, exams, treatments, procedures, surgeries . . . the hours of discomfort she endured—the cold, wet, stiff, stinging sensations they left on her body—all came back to her at once. Woomi shuddered at the belated sense of debasement coming over her. They used Woomi's living body however they pleased. She wanted to know exactly what they had done. And let everyone know what had happened.

Most books, articles, lab reports, and research materials were available online for any researcher to access on their personal computers. But the man couldn't find anything on Woomi. The materials that weren't on the research center database were stored in a library in the third basement of the main building in a special format. The man didn't know what data was stored there, what the format was, or who had access to it. He had heard that several researchers had broken into the library but never made it out with the data they were looking for.

The man was sure that the files related to Woomi were kept in the library. His job was to get her there. After that, it was all up to Woomi—to crack the code, break the lock, or whatever it was she needed to do.

THE HILL BEHIND the main building was darker than Woomi had expected; most of the streetlights along the trail were turned off. Woomi felt her way forward and figured out distance and space by picking up on the texture of the dirt beneath her feet, the ringing of her footsteps, and the ambient noise around her. The sounds of the wind, leaves rolling on the ground, little fruits rattling. Something thin but scratchy cautiously dragging past her. Sweat drenched her from crown to temple. Her back was soaked.

When she reached the main building, she ran down the

parking lot ramp and entered through the basement door. She'd chosen a pair of shoes with thin soles to minimize the sound of her footsteps, and her feet were already sore. The tingling pains that started when she was making her way over the hill had become intense, like having a nail driven into her foot each time she took a step. When she saw the sign for B3 in the stairwell, she plopped down on the landing. With her enormous hands, she massaged her feet through the shoes, thought to herself that her feet were too big. It was burdensome to have such big feet, baffling that a pair of feet this thick and strong-looking were killing her, and frightening not knowing where she might end up taking her final steps.

She tried sitting with her knees drawn up, but her thighs were too thick, so she leaned uncomfortably against the steps. Woomi couldn't say for certain why she was crying, but the teardrops grew heavier and her nose ran. Both hands cupped over her mouth to stifle the cries, she couldn't wipe her face. The green light of the floor sign refracted through her tears and turned to yellow, white, and light green. Woomi pushed herself up by pressing down on her knees, and walked into the overlapping circles of light.

The man's security card could not open the door to the third-floor basement. The researcher had said that the power room would cut off electricity at an agreed-upon time, at which point the security systems would also temporarily shut down. But the backup generator would kick in almost immediately and the door would lock again. All they had was maybe one second. She had to push the door and get inside the moment she heard the buzzer. *Don't miss the chance, don't hesitate.* Woomi's heart rang in her ear—*thump, thump, thump.* Moments later, a small beep rang like a sigh of relief or resignation. Woomi quickly leaned against the door with the whole weight of her body. The large, heavy door opened.

On the other side of the door was the same type of camera and dot of red light she'd seen at the back gate. Woomi obscured the lens with a sheet of dark gray paper she'd brought with her. The monitor in the security room was divided into tiny windows, and hundreds of cameras sent input in turn, so she could go unnoticed if there wasn't a lot of movement. The man said that he had gone into other people's labs this way, too, and that the darkness inside a building at night looked more or less the same everywhere.

Woomi shut her eyes tight and waited for nothing to happen. Sirens blared and all the lights came on in her mind. She shut her eyes tighter and slowly counted to sixty. Nothing happened.

The security team would help with the back gate, the power room would help with the door on the third basement level, and the researcher on call would help her get out of the parking lot, and when she was leaving the building . . . the man had recited the itinerary dryly. Woomi had asked why they were helping her. He asked, "Why do you think these people are helping you?"

"Are they against what the research center is up to?"

Brief silence.

"The security guard and the electrician said they feel sorry for you. The on-call researcher feels sorry for everyone in your shoes, that's all."

"And you?"

"Before I met you I had a vague sense of responsibility, or maybe guilt. But now, I feel the same way. I feel sorry for you. It's the outright and the specific that move people. Belief, in itself, has no power."

GLASS DOORS LINED both sides of the hall like a shopping arcade. It was too dark to see. Woomi trod slowly so as to not make a sound. Small rooms about the size of bathrooms sat behind glass doors, and in each room was a bed, and in each bed a person. Some lay on their backs with their hands on their chests, others lay on their sides with their legs crossed, and still others tossed about. When one of the glass doors opened soundlessly, Woomi stood in place, shifting from foot to foot, unable to advance or retreat. A silhouette much smaller than Woomi had stepped out and was looking at her.

"Isn't this . . . the library?" Woomi asked like a lost tourist. The silhouette nodded coolly.

The intruder demanded to know, "Where are the books?"

"Woomi. One hundred eighty-eight centimeters tall. Weight taken every three months this year: ninety-seven, ninety-five, ninety-six, ninety-seven kilograms, no significant change. Born thirty years ago on July thirtieth, around three a.m. at the Saha Estates. The parents were native residents but weren't able to obtain citizenship; were living in Town on L2 visas when father died of infectious respiratory disease on May seventeenth, around ten p.m. Mother also contracted same disease during pregnancy but recovered completely. Died of hemorrhage during birth. The one and only case of fetus contracting the respiratory disease in utero without miscarrying naturally. Specimen in use for infectious respiratory disease vaccine and cure research, DNA mutation, human embryo cloning, artificial organ for transplantation. Should I continue?"

Woomi stumbled back, unable to speak. The silhouette rushed to her and grabbed her hand.

"Please take me with you."

This was how the library stored information. Current number of Data Storages was ninety-seven. Exceptional children were chosen from the orphanage, put through intensive training for several years, and placed in the library when they passed the test. Their job was to remember. They spent all day in a private study memorizing and memorizing the data they were given. When a Data Storage had memorized all the names, places, organizations, and numbers exactly, the documents and files were disposed of. The same information was stored in at least three others at any given time, and when access requests came in, the information was cross-referenced. In this stage, the accuracy of the Data Storage's memory came to light. When their level of accuracy dropped below a certain level, they couldn't take on work anymore. But they weren't released from the library, either. They already remembered too much.

The woman was twenty. She had been recruited at ten and came to the library at fourteen. In the beginning she enjoyed the work she did. The workplace was clean, comfortable, and safe, and the research center paid close attention to her health and physical condition. She had a sense of pride that she was not like the other L2s—she was chosen for a special, important task. She had no worries or complaints, and her accuracy level was naturally high. But she was now at risk of being retired.

"What is the retirement age for a Data Storage? Are you getting close?"

The woman shook her head. "This library format isn't very old, so no one is old enough to lose their capacity. Besides, you become more sophisticated and proficient with time. It's not a matter of memory or focus; an error occurs when emotion interferes."

She said it was painful to know so much and have to retain it all. But she believed remembering was something only humans could do. *Never forget. Fear oblivion*, she told herself as she suffered through it. The act of remembering, of testifying, of being a record, of relishing the joys and grieving the sorrows for a long time. But when she realized that her memories weren't being accessed fairly or used in productive ways, the woman's level of accuracy plummeted.

Squeezing Woomi's arm harder, she said, "Take me away from here, please."

Woomi also needed the data, which this woman embodied. In ten minutes the locks would open once again in reverse order, and Woomi had to get out of the research center before that happened. Could she get out with this woman? Woomi wasn't sure, but she threw the woman over her shoulder anyway.

Just then, a long siren blared and a din erupted in their surroundings. *Clack, clack* . . . The sound of automated locks activating came closer, but she couldn't tell if they were locking or unlocking. *Are they locking me in or freeing me?* Hugging the woman close to her chest, Woomi stumbled back until she hit a wall. The woman was warm against her and her fine, unkempt hair tickled Woomi's face. A faint scent of disinfectant rose from her each time she moved.

Woomi's vision grew dark. Standing at a dead end, she was oddly at peace. The speed of her thoughts halved and the cogs in her brain rattled and squeaked as they turned slowly like a broken windup doll. The hall spun.

WOOMI WAS THE official residents' representative of the Saha Estates. There was a great deal that required her attention, more than one would expect, but the compensation she received for her services wasn't enough to cover expenses. Saha was becoming run-down and more things needed fixing with each passing year, but many units weren't able to pay the maintenance fee.

In truth, "cab fare" was the main source of Woomi's income.

The first time she came to the research center without Granny Konnim accompanying her, Woomi nervously fiddled with her visitor's pass on the elevator ride down. *Can I act as coolly as Granny? Confident, polite, and natural when I take the cab fare? Take it, and then what? Fold it and shove it in my pocket? Put it away carefully in my bag? Or walk out fanning myself with the bills?*

"Take a cab home," said the desk clerk. As always, she handed Woomi an envelope when she returned her visitor's pass. Woomi took the envelope with both hands and bowed at the same time, then spun on her heel. Without putting it in her bag or opening the envelope to make sure it was all there, she ran. The run turned into a waddle, difficult as it was to keep balance with both hands awkwardly holding up the envelope in front of her. She waddled her way out the front gate and climbed into a cab. "Saha Estates, please," she said. The driver didn't ask for confirmation or look at Woomi through the mirror, but drove on.

Large, fuzzy balls of dust were whirling in the air outside the cab window. They looked like snowflakes or dandelion seeds. It was early summer—unlikely it was either of those things. One flake of dust briefly clung to the window, trembled, and flew off again. It was a pointy seed with brown hairs on the tip. Fruit of the sycamore?

The main street off the alley to the Saha Estates was lined with an endless row of sycamores. In the spring, fruit dense with seed and hairs hung from the branches like upside-down lollipops, and when Woomi was young, she went out with the Saha kids to pick the fruit. With it, they played "Bomb Game," which involved throwing the fruit hard against the ground and watching it explode into a cloud of fuzzy seeds. The kids would not stop even as they sneezed, rubbed their eyes, and wiped the clear snot dripping from their noses. Other kids crushed the seeds under their heels, while Woomi was able to crush them in her palms.

"Bomb Game" wasn't as common these days. The trees had been replaced because the sycamore seeds were allergens. To see a sycamore, people had to go to the park. So where were these seeds coming from now? Woomi thought maybe the seeds were from back in those days. From the fruits she threw and crushed. They didn't get to land anywhere, take root anywhere, endured years of wind, rain, and snow, to return to Woomi.

Only then did she open the envelope. There was enough for ten round-trip cab fares. She was relieved by the decent amount, and ashamed that she was relieved by it. In that brief moment, she felt relief, fear, shame, and resignation in succession. Granny Konnim also received cab fare, but she did not take the cab. Woomi now understood how she was clothed, fed, and raised by this woman, who only tended to the garden and looked after the children. Woomi's eyes stung and watered like the time she got a sycamore seed in her eye.

She'd lived on money she hadn't worked for. And she lived well. As she lived well, as she grew tall and her muscles grew hard and strong, her emotions didn't develop as they should have. She skipped the maturing stage and went straight to old. Old and frail at heart. Woomi was afraid of being trapped, but even more afraid of being cast out from the Estates.

AN ARMED WOMAN about Woomi's age and a younger-looking man slowly approached. The other Data Storages had been woken up and were being escorted out by one of the staff, and the woman clinging to Woomi was shaking as if she were about to die.

"Calm down," the woman said, holding up her open palms. "Put down the Data Storage." Woomi shook her head and pulled out a fountain pen from her back pocket. It was the only weapon she'd brought with her. On the outside, it looked just like a regular fountain pen, but when the cap came off, a ten-centimeter blade appeared where the nib of the pen should be. The old man had given it to her the summer before. It had been an unusually hot, dry summer. Remembering how the old man often complained about how his office sat right under the beating sun, Woomi stopped by the supermarket to get an iced coffee and a popsicle. The coffee was for the old man and the popsicle was for herself. When she offered the old man the iced coffee, he thanked her and guzzled the coffee while simultaneously throwing the popsicle in his freezer. Woomi just laughed.

The old man and Woomi discussed trash collection, cleaning the first floor, and repairs around the Estates. Woomi suggested they stack bricks in between the railings and seal them with cement, and the old man had a hard time understanding. Woomi grabbed the nearest pen on the desk and opened the cap to draw him a picture. A blade appeared. It was small but whetted thoroughly—neither a joke nor a threat.

"You peel apples with this?" Woomi asked.

"No, I eat apples with the peel on."

"Too cute for self-defense."

"It's not for defending myself."

Woomi pressed the side of the blade against the back of her hand—even an untrained person could inflict fatal injury on oneself with a blade this sharp.

"It's for sacrificing myself. When I've run out of ways to protect someone."

"Have you ever used it?"

The old man shook his head. Woomi carefully replaced the cap and put it down. The old man picked it up again and handed it to Woomi.

"Take it."

"You don't need it?"

"I would like you kids to use it."

When she took out the fountain pen, the woman and man drew their guns at once and aimed at Woomi. The cap in her right hand, Woomi pulled the bottom off with her teeth. *Why didn't he say "you"? Why "you kids"?*

"Stay back." Woomi raised the knife to her throat. She wasn't going to go through with this implied threat, but her eyes filled with tears. Her vision undulated like a dream, a fantasy.

CURLED UP AS tight as she could go, Woomi was squeezed in even harder. A membrane as tough as rubber wrapped around her and filled with a thick liquid that went into her nose and throat, suffocating her. *I want to see for myself where I am. I want to cry for help. But if I open my eyes the liquid will rush into them, and if I open my mouth the liquid will fill my lungs. So I can't open my eyes or speak.*

The liquid filled Woomi's nose and started to make its way into her throat. As she held her breath, the liquid continued to push its way into her lungs, and Woomi gave in and swallowed the liquid in great gulps. She hiccupped from taking in too much at a time. After a hiccup so violent it jolted her entire person, she wasn't suffocating anymore. Her nose and mouth were still filled with sticky liquid, but she didn't feel uncomfortable. It felt as if she were breathing. *Did a pair of gills hidden somewhere on my body open up?* She wanted to feel around for them, but the membrane kept her movement constricted. *Hic. Hic.* She shook as she screwed up her courage and opened her eyes. Orange light poured in, burning them.

A face with soft lines looked down at Woomi. The very first moment of Woomi's life came back to her. Granny Konnim. Looking at her fearfully.

"Granny?"

The face that was gazing down at Woomi turned away and left.

"Mama?"

No one answered. Woomi didn't have the strength to lift her arm, and couldn't move her body at all. Another hiccup came out painfully as if tearing its way through her throat. Woomi could not stop groaning in agony until the next hiccup. Hiccup, groan. Hiccup, groan . . . She closed her eyes and thought, *I want to go back. To a time when I swallowed sticky liquid. A time when hiccups didn't hurt my throat. When my gills were open.*

TAP, TAP. A GENTLE, ringing knock. It was as close and loud as if someone were tapping on her head, but Woomi didn't feel anything. Eyes half-open, she looked around. A middle-age researcher in a lab coat. Young researchers in similar coats called him "Team Leader."

Woomi's last memory was of throwing the Data Storage woman over her shoulder. While she had been preoccupied with the man in front of her, someone else had come at her from behind. She had swung the knife reflexively but all it did was graze the man's neck. Woomi tried to sit up now, but she couldn't control her body.

"Are you all right?"

The Team Leader's voice felt far away. His face appeared over her, warping and stretching as if underwater. When the Team Leader softly plopped his hand over her face, Woomi saw that she was lying inside a transparent glass coffin. More hiccups.

"I'm thirsty."

"Hang in there. You're in the middle of surgery."

"I can't move my body."

"You're under anesthesia."

Woomi surveyed the glass coffin surrounding her. "What is this?"

"A clean room," the Team Leader answered curtly, and turned to a woman nearby. "I say we put her to sleep."

The woman nodded and picked up a syringe from a tray.

"Wait!" Woomi shouted. "I'm not sick!"

The Team Leader looked down at Woomi. She couldn't read his face through the curve of the glass pane.

"No, you aren't sick. And we're dying to know why. So we wanted to keep examining you until we found out, but you had to go and do something stupid. We can't let you go as if nothing happened, and we can't make up a room for you here, either. So we're in a bit of a bind, too."

The woman stuck the needle in one of the many tubes going into Woomi, who shouted as she fought not to fade away.

"What if I kill myself? I'll bet you still need me!"

She shouted a few more times. *Let me out, let me go, I'll kill myself.* A repulsive taste of medication rushed up from her esophagus and spread in her mouth, making her mute. The words that couldn't get out burrowed into Woomi's dream like kittens and mewed. The meowing was so frail and woeful that Woomi was overwhelmed with sadness even though she knew it was a dream.

Tears rolled down Woomi's face, and the Team Leader ran his hand over the glass as if wiping them away. "We can't lose you like this," he said. "There's still so much you need to show us. We've come this far. It'll be a shame to let go now."

JIN-KYUNG, UNIT 701

Jin-kyung stood by the window and fiddled with the antenna of the radio. It wasn't receiving the right frequency, and a static that sounded like thin sheets of paper crumpling grew louder and softer with the movement of the antenna. The moment she found the position with the least amount of static, the news came on.

First item was of course the mysterious murder near Saha Estates. Autopsy revealed a staggering five kinds of sleep medications and sedatives, and the DNA found on the clothes and body of the victim matched that of suspect D, a Saha. The police investigators were looking for D, whom they suspected of drugging and sexually assaulting the victim, ultimately murdering her through an overdose. The incident had brought to light the crimes caused by the Saha population, the residents of the Saha Estates in particular . . .

Jin-kyung turned off the radio.

The period before the incident had probably been the most

peaceful time in Town history. The weather was sunny and adequately humid; it was just before monsoon season. The nightly news at the time covered topics such as the rising average height and weight of Town children, and how milk sales were inversely proportional to precipitation. But now Do-kyung's case was top news. A woman found dead in a car in a deserted park. Evidence of sexual assault. That's all it took to pique interest. Then someone came forward and testified that there was a man who stalked and harassed her, and that the man was a Saha. The story turned in a whole new direction.

Outcry and fear concerning the Saha Estates erupted. The Saha Estates was suddenly the hideout for criminals from all over the world. That the Saha Estates was the *hub* of drug and illegal firearms trafficking was not true as far as Jin-kyung could tell. The media made it sound as if catastrophe were nigh if Saha wasn't closed down and all the Sahas in Town deported immediately, resulting in the Buildings Department and Resident Services opening an emergency investigation.

DRY, COARSE BRANCHES reached their arms at Jin-kyung. She backed away, but the branches grew fast and began following her. She didn't find the pursuit strange. It seemed as natural as water flowing down a mountain, and flower petals drifting in the spring breeze. The long, thick branches wrapped around Jin-kyung's wrists and ankles, her neck and waist. They tousled her hair, covered her eyes, passed between her legs. She knew that the tree had no emotions, no will nor intention, yet she was offended. It was demeaning. Jin-kyung snapped off the branches and freed herself, but they only restrained her more savagely, clawing her skin raw. She could hardly move.

Clearing the branches alone wasn't going to solve anything. Jin-kyung dug up the earth with her bare hands to uproot the trees altogether. Coarse, hard grains of sand got under her nails. Her fingertips ached. The pain was so intense she forgot about the scratches and the vine around her neck beginning to cut off the air.

A hard root the size of a human ankle was finally exposed and Jin-kyung couldn't believe how clean it was, how there were no root hairs, no dirt, no scratches. Deeper, deeper. She kept digging toward the tip, and found the root was bent. Like an elbow or a knee, it was unequivocally bent and heading straight up toward the ground. *What? What can this be?* Jin-kyung pressed her palms against the slick root. It was warm. She sensed movement. Not a large range of motion, but like the involuntary, regular movement of a cardiac muscle—a fine vibration, tremor, flexing.

She grabbed the root with both hands and pulled. The root that came up, overturning the earth around it, was Jin-kyung's leg. Two legs buried in the earth. Body unable to move. A tree that grows by feeding on itself. The branches entwining and fettering themselves.

As soon as Jin-kyung awoke screaming, she felt for her feet. Hard, callused soles, long toes, thick, bumpy toenails. She curled up into a ball, grabbed both feet in her hands, rolled over, and got up. Just then, her front door rattled. Not sure if it was a knock, she waited and listened. There was a sweeping sound. Unlike the first short, defined ring of something hitting the door, this was a long, faint scratching. Jin-kyung ran to the door and threw it open.

It was too early in the morning. There was no one at the door, and the sensors in the walkway were all off. She leaned over the railing and looked down at the yard just in case, but saw no one. A strange chill overtook her. Sensing a pair of hostile eyes glaring at her from somewhere in the dark, Jin-kyung was slowly turning when she felt something under her thin flip-flop soles. It was a pebble. A small, round pebble about the size of a thumbnail. Picked out specially from Granny Konnim's garden.

The sensor suddenly flashed on at the end of the walkway, and something heavy hit Jin-kyung in the arm. A patter of feet running down the steps followed. Before she could suspect or guess at anything, Jin-kyung reflexively started running after the footsteps. She flew down the flights of stairs, two, three, four steps at a time, caught him, and held him up by the scruff of his neck. It was Wooyon.

"What the hell?"

"Get lost."

"What?"

"Stop making things hard for Saha people—*get lost*."

She would often pass by the faucets, the garden, the garbage heap. Every time, Wooyon would wipe the expression from his face and look away at a far-off spot somewhere, clearly upset. He was well-behaved toward only Woomi— *Nuna*, he called her—and unless the person in question was about Granny Konnim's age or the old man's age, he spoke and behaved rudely.

"It's your fault! Find Nuna!"

Jin-kyung gently let go of his shirt. Woomi had been gone for three days. Jin-kyung was just as worried, but allowed Wooyon to take his anger out on her. He glared at Jin-kyung for a long time, spat on the ground, and turned on his heel.

Jin-kyung walked absent-mindedly down the walkways and ended up on the first floor. Granny Konnim was fetching water in the middle of the night. She'd filled the first container and was filling another. Jin-kyung dashed to her side and intervened.

"I told you not to fetch water on your own. Ask me or—"

She wanted to say Woomi's name but stopped herself.

"From now on, ask me."

The old man was the last person to see Woomi. It had been late in the evening. Woomi was walking out the gate past the Saha Estates sign, then suddenly turned around and came up to the custodian's office. She knocked on the window and asked him what the date was. The old man held up his desk calendar instead of answering.

"I've lived thirty years already," she said.

The comment was so out-of-the-blue that the old man wondered if he'd heard correctly. In the meantime, Woomi walked out of the gate and never came back.

This wasn't the first time Woomi left Saha without a word and didn't return for several days. She'd stayed out overnight countless times and returned saying she was at the police station, the lockup, or the research center; she once came back after three days and said she had been on a trip, and was once gone for a week to receive treatment because she wasn't feeling well. But this time, people's reactions were different. The old man turned the place inside out looking for her, saying she hadn't looked like herself when she left, but then stopped searching and fell silent all of a sudden. Granny Konnim locked herself up in her apartment. This made Jin-kyung nervous.

"Where is Woomi?" Jin-kyung asked Granny Konnim.

"You're asking me?"

"I'm asking you, Granny."

"Why don't you know? Why are you asking me?"

Why don't you know? Why? Why not? Why, why don't you know? For heaven's sake, why, why, why, why don't you know? Granny Konnim muttered the same thing over and over like a drunk. Jin-kyung thought at first that she was mocking her: *Why are you pretending you don't know?* Then it sounded like an accusation of neglect for not keeping track, then it sounded like Granny Konnim genuinely wanted to know why Jin-kyung didn't know where Woomi was.

"Woomi, is that you?" the old man cried, throwing his office door open.

The old man must have mistaken Jin-kyung's voice for Woomi's. Sunken eyes and cheeks. He'd become more haggard lately. His eyes were so filled with distress and sadness that Jin-kyung couldn't bring herself to correct him. As she stood not knowing what to say, the old man pressed hard against his temples and said, "I thought I heard her."

Jin-kyung slowly shook her head, and the old man fell to his knees, his legs giving out under him. Without a wail, without tears, he tore at his heart. As though Woomi had already been lost. Jin-kyung held her hand out to the old man. He swatted it away and stumbled back into his office.

After helping Granny Konnim into her house, Jin-kyung came back out into the yard. As she smoked, she thought of Woomi. As she climbed the stairs to her apartment, she thought of Woomi. As she lay alone in the empty apartment, she thought of Woomi. Woomi's big-knuckled hands and large, uneven front teeth. Woomi's heavy brow ridge and cheekbones. Thinking of Woomi, Jin-kyung found it hard to breathe evenly. She tried to take a deep inhale, but the air rolled in and rolled out against her will. Struggling to catch her breath, Jin-kyung tore at her chest like the old man and thought of Woomi, then of Do-kyung.

THE POSTMAN GRUDGINGLY knocked on the window of the custodian's office.

"You folks have mailboxes here?"

The old man was at a loss. The mailboxes had been filled with trash for a while and in time rusted shut. This was the first official mail to be delivered to the Saha Estates in the history of Town.

The old man came out of the office as he mumbled, "No mailboxes . . ."

"Then does mail go straight to the units?"

"Which unit is that for?"

"Seven-oh-one."

The old man looked up at the seventh floor thoughtfully and said, "Leave it here. I'll pass it on."

"It's express mail. You have to deliver it quickly."

The postman eagerly handed the envelope over to the old man, bowed, and rushed out of the gate. The old man turned over the envelope anxiously and felt his shoulders seize up the moment he saw who it was from.

The old man climbed the stairs with the envelope in his back pocket. What was to come was so daunting and suffocating he counted his steps to steel himself: 113, 114, 115, 116 . . . He thought of Jin-kyung and Do-kyung, who had climbed up and down more than a hundred steps every day. He thought of Su. Taking his time up to the seventh floor on his rounds as custodian was completely different from going straight up to Unit 701. He imagined climbing all those stairs would be no small task for young people, either, but he had never known just how painful and taxing it was. Climbing the stairs, the old man gained insight into another part of Jin-kyung.

The old man hesitated in front of Unit 701 for some time. When Jin-kyung opened the door, he handed her the envelope with as inscrutable an expression as he could manage, trying not to get ahead of himself when he didn't know what the envelope contained. Jin-kyung checked the contents, then looked at a faraway spot and slowly fanned herself with the envelope. The air moved languidly. Jin-kyung was expressionless and the old man waited patiently. Just then, a baby's cry came from Building B. But there was no baby at Saha.

"There must be a kitten somewhere," Jin-kyung said.

"It's a cat in heat."

"A kitten in heat?"

"So probably not a kitten."

"Then what is it?"

"Jin-kyung."

"Why does it cry like a kitten when it's not a kitten? Why does it go into heat whenever wherever and then cry like a poor little baby? Did you see it yourself? Did you check for yourself if it's a cat in heat or a kitten?"

News of Do-kyung's arrest and execution came so simply. Following the article under Saha and L2 criminal penalty enforcement, the remains were hygienically disposed of. Jin-kyung squeezed the envelope in her small hand and the sound of crumpling paper rang noisily down the quiet walkway. It sounded like a brittle sheet of glass breaking. Jin-kyung pushed the old man out of the way and ran down the stairs three, four steps at a time.

THE PARK RANGERS must have stopped making rounds at the park, for the place was overrun with weeds that hid the trails, and bits of garbage were wedged between every rock. The sour stench of rot carried in the wind. Swarms of winged insects. Jin-kyung lay down on the bench at the top of the stairs—the same ones she came up right after the incident, looking for her brother. Darkness gently shrouded the area. Time and space felt irrelevant. She was not sad. She was angry, numb, daunted, and completely helpless. She knew she was awake, but felt she was in a dream. She reached up to something crawling across her temples, and realized it was tears.

Someone called Jin-kyung's name. *Could this be a dream?* The second time it called, the voice was louder and clearer, prompting Jin-kyung to hide herself behind the bench and shout, "Don't come any closer."

But the person behind the voice came closer. At Jin-kyung's back was a steep cliff, and this stranger was closing in on her. Jin-kyung knew not to make any impulsive move.

"That's funny. I hear your brother was caught like this, too."

Jin-kyung could imagine Do-kyung standing paralyzed in a dead-end street. Do-kyung always had trouble making up his mind in the most crucial moments. Jin-kyung was always right there to give him the signal: *Go. Stop. Run.* The first steps Do-kyung took without Jin-kyung's guidance led him to Su. Jin-kyung hadn't realized until this moment just how significant those steps were. *Anyway, I hope you have no regrets. There are so many who spend their entire lives without taking a single step of their own volition.*

A woman whose face was obscured by two men with broad shoulders suggested Jin-kyung come to the research center with them.

"They have something they want to tell you."

"Would knowing change anything?"

"How should I know?"

"Then what's the point?"

The woman yawned and answered, "Don't ask me. That's for you to decide. But I'll tell you this: you'll follow me anyway. Maybe nothing will change, but there are still things you want to know. Nothing inspires action like curiosity, you know."

JIN-KYUNG FOLLOWED THEM down a long hall without saying a word. The hall was light gray from floor to ceiling, with identical windows at regular intervals; the monotony gave her vertigo. She thought about Woomi walking these halls. Woomi at five, clinging to Granny Konnim's hand; Woomi at fifteen, wishing she could run away; Woomi at twenty-five, resigned. Walking these halls for decades would have been tantamount to being hypnotized.

The windowless room they led her to was chilly. Like a room dipped in formaldehyde, it was clean but wet and unpleasant. The hum of the machinery ringing in her head grew louder on the right side, then left, and back and forth. Jin-kyung had to turn her head this way and that to put up with the noise.

By the door was a wooden table without decoration or pattern. Large enough for eight people, four on each side. A middle-age man was seated at the far end of the table drinking from a teacup. There wasn't any steam rising from the teacup with a long, slender handle; an identical cup was placed across from him as if to say, *Sit here.* It was water. Behind the table were four or five stainless steel lab tables. The room didn't seem like a place for entertaining guests. *A lab? Why did they bring me here?* Jin-kyung's right eye fluttered. Her heart fluttered even more rapidly. She was about to reluctantly take a seat when she saw something under the glass cover of the lab table.

It was no ordinary lab table. A glass pane covered a display case like at the butcher's, and there was something inside. Jin-kyung was frightened and nervous, but curious. She wanted to confirm with her own eyes, but at the same time did not want to look. She remembered what the woman had said. Nothing motivates a person like curiosity.

Jin-kyung walked up to the lab table and looked. Woomi.

She was covered in gauze from chest to thighs, but the gauze was so thin the contours of her body and hair showed through. Face so white as to be blue, lifeless lips, eyes half-open and showing only whites. Woomi lay before her eyes. Jin-kyung felt sick. She cupped her hands over her mouth to stop herself from retching.

"I don't want to talk in this room," said Jin-kyung.

The man frowned. Three straight wrinkles appeared between his brow.

"We brought you to our lab because we couldn't think of anywhere else. No better place than this to have a quiet conversation, too."

The man took a sip of water and continued, "Wouldn't it be better for the both of us to get this over and done with?"

He gestured at the seat across from him, and Jin-kyung leaned her hands against the table as she sat down. She was thirsty, but she didn't drink the water they had prepared for her. Something kept gushing up from within. The feelings she'd been repressing came out all at once. A helplessness as great as her rage, the guilt it brought, and the layers of questions and exhaustion wrapped around her like a chrysalis. And in the last moment, the winged creature that ripped the shell apart and sprang forth wasn't a butterfly but a moth. The moth scattered filthy dust as it flapped its heavy wings. Jin-kyung jumped at the man, knocking him over. She shook him by the collar.

"Why did you have to take it this far? Why?"

The man shoved Jin-kyung aside, his expression irritated. "Not dead."

"What?"

"Not dead."

Jin-kyung thought of Do-kyung. Then she lifted her head and looked at Woomi. Eyes half closed. She thought she saw Woomi's lips twitch. Jin-kyung couldn't bring herself to ask whom he was talking about. She couldn't bear to weigh the value of the two lives. Jin-kyung released the man; he dusted his shirt indifferently and picked the chair back up. Back in his seat, he lazily traced the smooth rim of his teacup with the tip of his finger and added, "Not dead. Either of them. Not yet, anyway."

A storm raged inside Jin-kyung's head. Unmoved, the man kept his eyes lowered. Jin-kyung licked her lips several times, but her tongue was too sticky and dry to wet her lips. She picked up the teacup from the table and took a sip. Water made its way to every papilla like an ocean wave crashing at sandcastles. The tense muscles in her mouth and on her tongue relaxed.

Jin-kyung licked her lips with her moistened tongue and asked, "Do-kyung. Is he here, too?"

"No, but we can help you, I think."

"With what?"

"What you want."

"Why?"

"Quid pro quo, maybe."

The man ambled around to the back of the lab table. He placed his hand on the glass above Woomi and ran his hand across the pane as if to caress her face.

"She was the first project I got after I finished my apprenticeship. Something possessed the head researcher at the time to steal all her records and vanish, so she pretty much fell in my lap. It took a lot of time and work to get the lab in order and patiently fill the blanks in the research."

The man's thick eyebrows twitched several times. Flashes of murderous rage appeared in his eyes as he gazed intently at Woomi. Jin-kyung saw an unnerving excitement in them. The prince who fell in love at first sight with the princess lying in the glass coffin, who begs the dwarves to let him take her. Dead princess. Dead and lying in a glass coffin. A large, pale woman asleep like a princess who was careless enough to bite into an apple from a stranger, and then fell unconscious. What did the prince plan to do with her body? If the coffin hadn't slipped from the manservant's hand, if the piece of apple lodged in her throat hadn't popped out on impact, if the princess had never woken up. Perhaps the prince would have chosen an ending in which the princess stayed in eternal sleep, with no happily ever after.

Jin-kyung was silently cradling her cup when Woomi opened her eyes. Her pale lips parted a bit to take a deep, slow breath, which clung white on the glass pane and disappeared instantly. Woomi closed her eyes again. She was alive. Woomi. Really and truly. Alive.

"What do you want?" Jin-kyung asked.

The man took a sip of his water so as not to appear desperate. "There's some material we need. It's at Saha, with someone who lives there. We'd like you to convince this person to turn the material over to us."

"Why don't you go ask yourself?"

ore ero e.a

"We tried. Didn't work. Threatened to burn it."

"What is it? And who has it? And why are you asking me?"

"I think you'll be able to deliver."

"Why me?"

"Because we have something you want."

It dawned on Jin-kyung that she wouldn't be able to refuse him.

"And you'll help me?" she asked.

"I'm not saying I'll do anything myself. I have no power."

"Then who?"

"How should I know? No one knows. Someone far away and powerful that no one knows about. A group of someones."

The man produced a business card from his pocket and slid it across the table.

"Think about it and call me. The sooner, the better. Patience is not a strength of mine."

JIN-KYUNG HAD TO push past a sea of people arriving for work as she exited the research center. She did not have a single coin on her. She watched a crowd of children in uniforms get off at a bus stop. A group of boys in gray cotton pants and white shirts got off first, followed by girls in skirts and blouses of the same palette. The boys pulled at each other's bags, shouldered each other, and rushed on ahead, while one boy hung back leaning against the bus stop sign. The girl who was last to get off the bus went to his side. They walked a little ways behind the crowd. They didn't hold hands, speak, or look at each other. They only walked side by side, eyes ahead.

The cherry trees planted along the path made a tunnel

overhead, their branches hanging heavy with green leaves. When the leaves caught the sunlight they looked emerald, white, and even gold. The young couple walked along the sun-dappled cherry tree tunnel. *Never knew the beauty of the summer cherry trees after the flowers and the fruits have come and gone. Never knew the yearning of spring, the glittering summer, the warmth of autumn, the subdued winter. Never knew anything at all. Can't say I lived at all. Can't say this is living,* Jin-kyung thought.

THE OLD MAN was watering the garden with a hose. As she came in through the gate, Jin-kyung acknowledged him with a nod as if nothing had happened. The old man regarded Jin-kyung for a moment and clapped his hands together to dry them. The faucet shut off with the throaty sound of choking back tears, and the old man's hands looked rough even when dripping. As if agreed upon in advance, neither spoke of Do-kyung.

"Did you see Woomi?" the old man asked. Jin-kyung didn't answer because she couldn't figure out the real purpose behind the question, and the old man dragged his feet back into the office. Jin-kyung was confused. Did he know something?

Jin-kyung looked around at the ruined garden. Desiccated stalks and leaves crumbled at her fingertips like the wings of a pinned butterfly. *Will they be revived? Buds and leaves come in again, bloom flowers, bear fruit?* Granny Konnim would pick the fruits and vegetables straight off the plants and give them to Jin-kyung. Cherry tomatoes, cucumbers, lettuce, sesame leaves, and bomdong flowers.

Whatever Granny Konnim gave her, Jin-kyung popped in her mouth right away without washing or even dusting off the dirt. Sweet, juicy, aromatic. Sometimes smooth, sometimes scratchy on her tongue, crisp in texture. She'd once bitten into a hot pepper without realizing and wept. Watching Jin-kyung guzzle water with her mouth on the faucet, Granny Konnim had giggled—*hehehehe!*—like a child. In all the time Jin-kyung had known Granny Konnim, that was the only time she'd heard her laugh.

Jin-kyung thought about going upstairs but instead went into the custodian's office. She and the old man sat side by side in front of the small TV. She ran her thumb over the corners of the business card inside her pocket as she thought about Woomi. Gigantic Woomi lying as if dead. The white breath from Woomi's lips. Do-kyung—was he really alive? Jin-kyung was too afraid to make up her mind.

When the news came on, the old man turned up the volume. The Saha Estates was scheduled to be demolished. The Council of Ministers had decided to crack down on the recent major crimes around the Saha Estates and to launch a downtown redevelopment project. Squatters were expected to vacate the premises voluntarily by the end of the month, and forced eviction would begin on the second of the following month.

Most of the Saha people would have heard the news, but no one said a word. It was a quiet evening like most evenings at Saha, and the old man and Jin-kyung were each deep in their own thoughts.

"Jin-kyung . . ." the old man suddenly said. "Never mind." He called her again and changed his mind again.

Jin-kyung left the office and smoked in a corner of the garden. She pulled out the business card and examined the back and front. Was it delusional to think that the announcement to demolish Saha was their way of pressuring, threatening Jin-kyung? Just then, someone came up from behind and snatched the business card from her hand. She whipped her head around in surprise and saw the old man squinting at the card. Was she allowed to show it to others? Jin-kyung wondered for a moment, but all it contained was a number anyway.

"Who?"

Jin-kyung only laughed, not knowing what to tell him.

The old man shrugged. "You know the story of the turtle and the hare?" he asked, returning the business card to her.

"The race? Hare falls asleep?"

"That's the tortoise and the hare. Turtle. I'm talking about the turtle."

The old man settled into the chair in front of the custodian's office and began the story. Once, long, long ago, the Dragon King, who lived in the Dragon Palace in the ocean, was fatally ill, and . . . Jin-kyung was bewildered by how serious the old man was about this story. He paid no attention to Jin-kyung as he did voices of different characters as if he were acting out a children's story for an audience of one. The only cure for the Dragon King's illness was the famous rabbit liver. So after a rumble and tumble the turtle brings the rabbit to the Dragon King, but the rabbit lies: "I left my liver out in the sun to dry." So the turtle swims back to land with the rabbit.

"You think it was wrong of the rabbit to lie?" the old man asked.

"It was scared blind. Its life depended on it."

"That's right. That's why you never trust the words of someone who's scared blind. It wasn't there. He followed all the way back, but the liver still wasn't there. So always ask yourself, 'Where is the real thing?'"

Maybe he did know something, the old man. Jin-kyung took out a cigarette and gave it to him. He waved it off and went back into his office. Jin-kyung took his seat and mulled for a long time over what he said.

It wasn't there. He followed all the way back, but it still wasn't there. So always ask yourself, "Where is the real thing?"

THE OLD LADY at the temp agency slowly rose from her desk, pushing her chair back. She limped over to the door and bolted the lock. The metal parts clanked. Something within Jin-kyung collided as well.

The agent sat down on the sofa in the middle of the office, as if putting down the weight of her body and soul. The sofa sighed in response. The agent pointed at the sofa across from her with her chin as if to say, *Come, sit.* Jin-kyung kept her back straight so as not to betray her unease, and sat on the sofa. The agent pulled out a silver cigarette case from under the desk with shaking hands. There were eight thin cigarettes lying side by side, and the agent picked up one, held it upside down, and tapped it on the surface of the table. Jin-kyung quickly pulled out a disposable lighter from her pocket and politely offered her a light, protecting the flame with her free hand. The agent's wholly satisfied grin looked almost like a grimace.

She pushed the cigarette deep in her mouth for a drag,

leaving the filter soaking and filthy with lipstick she'd applied and reapplied many times over the course of the day. The agent blew out a long, long plume of smoke as if intent on breathing out every last breath of soul that resided in her. The ashtray contained half a dozen butts crushed at the waist that all bore the same shade of lipstick stain. The agent added another butt to the congregation. Then she reached inside her pocket to pull out a tube of lipstick and sedulously repainted her lips. Jin-kyung quietly attended her ritual. The agent gently rubbed her lips together a few times, creating deep, pretty pink wrinkles on her lips.

"You," she said. "How do you know you can trust me with the information you just blabbed?"

"I don't trust you."

"What were you thinking, then?"

"I thought if anyone could get ahold of one, it would be you, ma'am."

"What's it for?"

"I'm gonna kill them all."

The agent wasn't amused or surprised.

"Ever used one?"

Jin-kyung couldn't answer.

The agent pulled out a memo pad from under the table, plucked the expensive fountain pen from her breast pocket, and slowly wrote down an address.

"Go there. I'll make a call."

The right side of the agent's face twitched. The involuntary movement made the deep oblong scar under her eye open and close.

Jin-kyung bowed at her and was about to go when the agent asked, "Aren't you gonna pay?"

"Oh, how much is it?"

"Does it matter? Do you have it?"

Jin-kyung couldn't answer but rubbed one corner of the piece of paper between her fingers. The agent pulled out another cigarette with her shaking hands.

"Until you pay it off, I'm taking all of your pay. So until you do, don't rest, don't pick and choose, just take all the jobs I assign you."

The agent took out another cigarette and a slim gold lighter from her cigarette case. She flicked the lighter, but there was no spark. Jin-kyung watched for a moment as the agent wrestled the small lighter that must have glittered at some point but was now so scratched up and worn it had lost most of its luster, and took out her disposable lighter again. The agent waved her off.

Some things we want to take care of ourselves, trivial little things that we do, not because we're bored, but to get a break from the work and the fear. Opening a jar that won't budge. Peeling a sticker that won't come off clean. Untangling a knot in an odd place. Jin-kyung wondered if lighting her own cigarette meant something like that to the agent.

THE OFFICE OF MINISTERS, where the seven ministers handle their official business, is located on the property of the Parliament Building. That's what people say, but it's not an uncontestable fact. The Office of Ministers is a run-down three-story building. Following the opinions of the founding ministers that having a separate building for themselves was a waste, the Office of the Ministers takes up as little space as possible in the Parliament Building. The work brings no wealth or glory, which leaves them with only pride and duty. Shrouded identities, enormous power, a life of sacrifice and no reward. The ministers had the respect and gratitude of their Citizens. They believed Town was the safest, wealthiest country with the highest quality of life thanks to their own flawless judgment. Town did not waste time on trial-and-error or taking opinion polls.

The stock footage for news related to the Council of Ministers was always one and the same. It was a poor-quality video possibly shot decades ago. It showed an empty conference room with a large, circular conference table and seven black chairs with high backs. Seven microphones at the chairs, seven water glasses. A fancy chandelier that seemed out of place. Only one of the seven glasses was filled, which Jin-kyung found strange and always looked closely at every time the shot came on the news.

That was the only video of the Council of Ministers that was available to the public. Outsiders, including the press, were strictly prohibited from entering the Office of Ministers. The ministers refused all interviews, which gave rise to a host of rumors: that they were living a more plush life than they let on, or that their office at the Parliament was a decoy and they really lived inside the research center, or that there was a tiny island that doesn't even appear on maps, and that was the ministers' paradise. A former research center director who was supposedly dead had really assumed the position of minister. A famous film actor was moonlighting as a minister. There was no evidence to support any of these rumors.

THE MINISTERS HAD their daily meeting at two in the afternoon, and Jin-kyung was scheduled for a visit as a representative from a teen educational excursion business. The agent arranged it all. In the yellow envelope she gave Jin-kyung was a brochure for a teen educational excursion program and a visit application.

"You are a staff member at the company and you'll be going on a field visit to the Parliament tomorrow. Your ID is in the envelope."

The agent gave her an old map and a few pictures of poor quality. The map, of unknown source, was a photocopy that was amended in many places with white-out and pen. Jin-kyung looked at the map she had no reason to believe was accurate as if determined to commit all of it to memory. One of the photographs was a satellite photo of the Parliament and Office of Ministers buildings. There were parts between the map and the photograph that did not overlap exactly. Jin-kyung thought there might be hidden bunkers or secret passageways.

Jin-kyung traced the map with her finger to go over the route. First, the visitors' center to sign in. There was an ID in the envelope with a fake name and, surprisingly, Jin-kyung's photo. *How did the old lady get a picture of me?*

Next came the security checkpoint. The guards check the contents of all bags and pockets. The only items that could be taken past that point without raising an alert were cell phones and cameras. Jin-kyung managed to fit a revolver in a thor-oughly hollowed-out camera. This was the first hurdle: get-ting past the visitors' center with the fake ID and the hidden revolver.

Once inside, she would be escorted by a guide who spe-cialized in field visits. Past the annex and into the main build-ing. A tour of the Assembly Hall and out the back door to look at the gardens, ditch the guide, and sneak into the Office of Ministers via the passage by the library. The passage in the satellite photo looked like a jungle. Untamed for a long time, or perhaps densely populated with tough, thorny plants on purpose, it was a dark green close to black, and there were no traces of foot traffic there. Jin-kyung told herself that it only looked like that because it was a low-quality satellite photo, but it was hard to shake off the fear that a path didn't exist and the building was not the Office of Ministers.

She chose a pair of pumps with low heels. Putting on a double-breasted linen jacket over an ordinary blouse, she thought of Woomi and Do-kyung. She thought of what the old man had said.

THE OFFICE OF MINISTERS

The drowsy-looking middle-age woman at the desk scanned the barcode on the ID, checked that it matched with the name on the visitor reservation, and robotically handed Jin-kyung a visitor's pass. Jin-kyung put her bag on the desk, along with the camera that couldn't take pictures and cell phone that would never ring. After her bag and jacket were inspected,

Jin-kyung slung the camera with a large barrel on her shoulder and slipped the phone in her back pocket.

The staffer who was to show her around wore high heels that made clearly defined footsteps. Jin-kyung slowed down her pace. In order not to seem nervous, she turned her head this way and that instead of just moving her eyes, all the while making levelheaded comparisons between the actual place and the route she had memorized.

FIRST STOP WAS the annex. They walked through the gallery where the history of the Parliament and Town from independence to present day could be surveyed in one place, and moved on to the Governing Experience Hall. Jin-kyung tried the power button on the microphone built into the desk, and pressed the buttons on the electronic voting system. The guide explained that the hall was a facility built recently to show students how to propose bills, vote, and pass laws. Then they headed to the main building to see the Assembly Hall.

The police officers on guard kept glancing at Jin-kyung, bothered by a young woman with a visitor's pass touring the Parliament on a weekday afternoon. Each time they looked at Jin-kyung, she covered her face with the camera, pretending to take a picture. A camera that was an empty shell. A viewfinder with no view. A shutter that clicked but took no pictures. A memory without record. Jin-kyung thought she was like the camera. She touched signs absentmindedly, peeked in through open doors, and turned doorknobs. The police frowned warily at her a few times, then assumed she simply had annoying habits, and stopped paying attention to her.

"I need to use the bathroom."

The bathroom sign peeked out at the end of the hall. The guide smiled at Jin-kyung and gestured for her to go. Jin-kyung maintained the same speed and gait all the way into the bathroom. She turned the faucet at one of the sinks ever so slightly so that water flowed in a steady trickle, checked to make sure all six stalls had the green vacant sign on, and went into the stall at the very end.

She'd rehearsed this all night. She opened the front of her jacket, which she'd only buttoned at the top, took it off, and hung it on the wall hook. She unhooked the camera strap to adjust the length, pulled the strap over her shoulder, and hooked the ends together at the chest. She took out the gun holster from the padded part of the camera strap. She pried the camera open, took out the revolver fitted in firmly at an angle, and put it in the holster. She wrapped the camera shell with toilet paper and tossed it in the garbage, and put her jacket back on. She buttoned the jacket with one hand, flushed with the other, and came out of the stall in about two minutes. The bathroom was still deserted and the faucet was still maintaining a very fine stream. Jin-kyung wet the tips of her fingers and turned the tap off.

A police officer ran into Jin-kyung as she was coming out of the bathroom, shaking the water off her hands. The officer frowned when some of the water splashed on him, and Jin-kyung grinned sheepishly and apologized. Watching Jin-kyung wipe her hands on her pants legs as she passed by, the officer grumbled, "Boorish woman."

Jin-kyung asked if the children would be allowed to see the garden, and the guide, as anticipated, led her out the back door.

"The garden is also available for tours, but honestly it isn't much to look at right now."

The Parliament garden was completely open to the public for only five days a year, during the Tulip Festival. Tulips of all colors filled the fifteen or so acres of the Parliament property, and children came in numbers greater than the tulips. Thanks to this festival, the tulip became the symbol of the Parliament and the Council of Ministers.

"Tulips don't have separate calyxes. The three petals on the inside are the original petals and the three on the outside are what used to be the calyx. The gentle lines and unique shape of the tulip made this flower a favorite among the European aristocracy."

Jin-kyung closed her eyes for a moment and pictured the garden filled with tulips of all sorts of vivid colors, like jelly beans filling up a jar. She could almost smell the sweetness. The festival was over and the tulips had all been cut and removed.

"Too bad there are no flowers."

"But a pond has been newly installed in the garden."

In front of the library was a pond that wasn't part of the map Jin-kyung had memorized. Jin-kyung followed one step behind the guide. She was getting closer to the Office of Ministers building and farther from the police officers guarding the garden entrance.

Rocks big and small were stacked around a pond about three meters wide. Jin-kyung stood up on top of a flat rock and looked down. The water was so clear that she could see the rocks and sand on the bottom, and there was no algae anywhere. A dozen red and yellow carp were gliding to and fro.

The carp were at least fifty centimeters long, but they were flat and had very little meat on them. If the pond had been some-place open to the public, the fish would have been fattened up on scraps from passersby. Jin-kyung came down from the rock and stood next to the guide.

"Can I feed them?"

"Oh, I'll find out if feeding the fish can be added to the program."

"No, I mean, right now."

"We have no fish food at the moment."

"I have some rusk with me. The carp are so skinny."

The guide only smiled awkwardly, not knowing what to do, and allowed it in the end. "Oh well, all right," she said.

Jin-kyung undid her top button and was slipping her right hand in her jacket when the guide suddenly cried, "Your camera's gone!"

Jin-kyung opened the second button with her left hand and grabbed the weapon, warmed by her body heat. The guide's eyes grew wide. Her mouth opened and drew a violent intake of air. *When she breathes out, a scream will come out with it.* Jin-kyung opened up the left flap of her jacket to hide the gun in her right hand from view, and shoved the barrel in the guide's solar plexus. The deafening gunshot sliced through the congealed air. The guide made a sound like air rushing out as she fell forward.

THE YOUNG MAN who was introduced as the agent's friend had given Jin-kyung a thorough tutorial.

"This right here is the barrel, or the muzzle. This is where the bullets come out. You know that, right?" he said. "The pointy thing up here is the gun sight. You want to align the target with the front bit and the back bit when you're aiming. This is the button you press to release the chamber, and the part that goes around and around is the chamber. Each time you take a shot, it moves one slot. And what do you call this? That's right—the trigger. You've seen this, right?"

This went on for a good five minutes. Then he demonstrated how to hold the gun, aim it, and minimize recoil. Jinkyung tried it herself, and he adjusted her form. The gun was heavier than it looked and strained her wrists.

"A Glock would be nicer, but beggars can't be choosers. This is pretty small and quiet, though, as far as revolvers go," he said, and pointed at a birdcage in a corner of the office. "Shoot that."

"Excuse me?"

"Try hitting the bigger of the two canaries over there."

"*Shoot* shoot?"

"You're just gonna go straight for the real thing without a practice run? This is your practice. Just one shot. Aim, hit."

Jin-kyung took a deep breath in and out. As the man taught her, she held the butt lightly in her hand, placed her index finger on the trigger, and steadied her right hand with the left. Yellow bird staring off as if deep in thought. Jin-kyung aligned the bird's tiny head with the front and back sight bits. She was strangely not nervous at all. She shut her eyes tight and opened them again. The bird hadn't moved. Jin-kyung slowly pulled her right index finger toward herself.

Click. The echo of an empty chamber revolving. There was no recoil or sound. *Hmm?* Jin-kyung lowered her arm and checked on the canary, and the man snickered.

"Good. You're all set. Good to go."

"Huh?"

"Practice over."

"Did I hit it? Did the bullet release?"

"The lady knows no fear, huh? You were really gonna shoot? You can't risk people hearing shots coming from here. The way you pulled the trigger like it's no big deal, you're good to go. You get exactly eight shots. Don't waste them, and good luck."

Jin-kyung wondered what would have happened if she'd really shot the canary. If the bullet had gone where she'd aimed, the bird would have been blown to bits. Would she really have been okay with that? Only then was she nervous, even frightened.

SO THIS WAS her first shot. Ears ringing and out of her wits, Jin-kyung ran along the dirt path between the library and the annex. *If I had done nothing, would the woman have screamed at the exhale? Would she have attacked me? I shot a person. A person who cordially showed me around, waited for me while I went to the bathroom, and gave me permission to feed rusks to the carp.* A hairline fracture appeared on Jin-kyung's iron heart and solid resolve.

At the end of the dirt path, a grove of randomly planted trees stood in her way. Avoiding the great trunks and trying to jump over wild weeds and vines, Jin-kyung fought to keep her balance as the stalks and creepers caught on her feet. She stumbled forward, broke the fall with her hand, and felt a sharp sting travel up her arm. A stray wire cut her palm and was lodged under her thumb. A gunshot rang behind her. She left the wire in her hand and ran.

The wound throbbed and the wire caught on her jacket. Jin-kyung stopped to yank it out with her front teeth. A tiny stream of blood spurted from her hand in a hyperbola. Jin-kyung reflexively sucked on the wound and tried to stop the bleeding with her tongue as she ran.

"Stop right there!"

Then came another shot, followed by a higher-pitched voice.

"Stop! Or I'll shoot!"

While Jin-kyung was struggling to pull the wire out, the pursuers had closed in significantly. They were likely the police officers who were guarding the back gate. Both of them were running after her, so apparently the guide had been left to die. She had hit her right in the stomach, and she was probably gone already, but the thought of the woman dying alone tormented Jin-kyung as she ran. Her limbs were heavy and the path was rough. She kept tripping and falling down, unable to advance much faster.

Stumbling over a bush, Jin-kyung felt an intense heat whiz past her ear with a sharp shriek. She ducked and looked back. One officer was busy jumping over the shrubbery as he made his way toward her, and the other was aiming at Jin-kyung with his shoulders in a tense knot. He seemed as inexperienced as Jin-kyung. His shoulders were drawn up too close to his ears, and his elbows were bent, nervously pulling the gun too close to his face. Jin-kyung aimed at him, then lowered her weapon. She figured neither of them could hit the other anyway.

Jin-kyung ran toward the Office of Ministers at full speed. A black gate held fast in the grasp of crawling vines appeared, and a shot Jin-kyung was certain wasn't aimed at her rang and scattered in the air.

An iron gate with bars as slender as fingers stood before her. The top of the gate was decorated with curls like locks of hair, and spearheads were placed intermittently. The gate was low and not so forbidding, as if it didn't mind intruders, and it was quiet on the other side. There were no security cameras that she could see. *Maybe it's electric?* Jin-kyung threw a branch at the gate, but nothing happened. Behind her, a new group of men were closing in. She had only one way out. Jin-kyung hopped over the gate. A bullet hit the gate and ricocheted.

JIN-KYUNG BLACKED OUT. She hadn't hit her head and wasn't electrocuted. She remembered landing softly on her right shoulder and rolling forward to reduce the impact, but a gap had opened up in her consciousness as if she'd been switched off and on. She found herself on top of something papery but cushy and damp.

Jin-kyung was lying faceup on a pile of leaves right by the iron gate she'd jumped over. The pile gave off an awful rotting stench, and a sinister dampness rose from it. On the other side of the gate, the men who were after her were walking away at a casual pace. *Why did they stop following me? That's so strange. Strange, but strangely conceivable.*

An old three-story building came into view in the distance. Jin-kyung placed her hand on the holster in her jacket.

WINDOWS OPEN AT various angles took up more than half the outer wall of the building. When the wind blew, some of the windows closed, others opened a little, and still others squeaked loudly without budging. The ones that had swung open knocked and rattled together. Vines crawled up the plastered walls and climbed inside the windowsills. Some had been pinched between the pane and the sill and cut off, but the ones that intertwined formed braids that kept the windows ajar, and creeped along the inside of the wall. These weren't windows that were left open; they were windows that could not shut.

There was no one inside. Only the wind, dried leaves, and sand came and went as they pleased through the open windows. The tension in Jin-kyung's shoulders eased as she circled the building, and the hand on the holster relaxed and fell to her side. When she returned to where she'd started, a fancy chandelier hanging from the middle of the ceiling came into view.

Among the dangling crystals, spiderwebs hung in a chaotic mess. The wind blew, and the webs billowed like strings of sugar in a cotton candy machine. Some of the flower-shaped bulbs in the sockets were broken. Jin-kyung doubted the ones that weren't broken would light up. It took a long while for Jin-kyung to remember the scene where this very chandelier had shone brighter and colder than the moon. It was on the television news. Large, round conference table, seven chairs, seven microphones, seven glasses, and the chandelier. Light refracted by hundreds of crystals streaming in all directions. Chandeliers were more decorative than functional, and used bulbs with low luminosity and warm color, and Jin-kyung remembered thinking that the bulbs weren't effective, as they were uncommonly white and too bright.

But it was just the chandelier. No table, no chairs, microphones, glasses. One small wooden chair in the corner, a badly smudged see-through glass elevator that led to who knew where if it worked at all, and at the center were the steps to the second floor. Dust, leaves, and scraps of paper rolled on the floorboards. Jin-kyung said softly to herself, "This can't be it. This can't be the conference room. This can't be the chandelier. Maybe this isn't the Office of Ministers."

Looking inside the building, Jin-kyung suddenly realized that there was no door. The walls held only windows. This was the ground floor, and yet there was no door. *What is this place?*

THE MOMENT JIN-KYUNG jumped into the building through a wide-open window, the elevator car in the glass shaft moved, shaking the entire building. In this strange painting of a place where time had stopped, Jin-kyung's appearance broke the spell and had time moving again. *Is this a dream? Am I in a dream?* Jin-kyung stomped on the wooden floor. The stomps echoed in the empty, high-ceilinged space. The sound came in through her ears and the reverberation traveled up her legs and throughout her body. *This is not a dream*, Jin-kyung told herself as she climbed the stairs.

The second floor was decorated like the lobby of a small hotel. There was a large marble table by the stairs and around it were leather couches, potted fortune plants, and some floor lamps without bulbs. The armrests of the couches were made of wood, but everything else was a dark clay-colored leather. Not very ornate but luxurious at a glance, the dusty sofa was seemingly well-preserved. It looked like it was hardly used, as the shine of the leather and the firmness of the cushion were still intact, and there were no scratches or tears. But it was old-fashioned. A literally old sofa. The circular carpet on the floor, the floor lamp, and the phone on the end table were all objects from another time.

Past the table was a wide, tall visitors' information desk, and behind it was a long hall with large wooden doors on each side with no signs. Down the end of the hall were the stairs to the third floor. Jin-kyung realized that the second floor didn't have the elevator she'd seen on the first floor.

Aiming her gun in turn at the doors along the hall, the stairs at the end of it, and back at the lobby, Jin-kyung carefully approached the first door. The knob didn't turn at all. She pushed and pulled, but it didn't budge. Jin-kyung lifted her foot high and kicked the door with her heel. The door didn't open, but the door and wall shook together. They were one piece. The door wasn't made to open up to another space. It was a decorative façade or a tromp l'oeil. All the other doors were the same.

Wind blew. Two large windows were open to the back of the lobby, and outside tall trees swayed idly in the breeze. A forest so overgrown in the Parliament garden, a building so old and peculiar in that forest—Jin-kyung couldn't believe it as she stood there. She reached the stairs at the end of the hall and went up to the third floor.

FOUR MACHINE GUNS with long barrels were waiting for Jin-kyung at the top of the stairs. Jin-kyung slowly opened her right hand, and the revolver landed hard on her foot. Jin-kyung kept climbing the steps with both hands open. The four gun barrels backed up slowly, maintaining the aim and distance.

"Stop."

The voice was muffled by a face mask, but it definitely belonged to a woman. Jin-kyung noticed that the one on the far right was smaller than the others. At the woman's signal, two approached Jin-kyung and frisked her meticulously for quite a long time. One of them had a particularly rude touch. When Jin-kyung slapped the hand touching her waist, the person backed away with palms up as Jin-kyung had done. The other person turned and nodded to confirm Jin-kyung was unarmed, at which point the others moved back to make way for her.

The third floor was uncannily small. Jin-kyung had noticed from the outside that the building was shaped like a pyramid, but she was surprised by how small this floor was compared to the second floor. On the ceiling was the same chandelier she saw on the first floor, traces where pillars used to be, an empty decorative mantelpiece, a roll of carpet gathering dust in the corner, and windows, some open and some broken. At the far end of the hall was a pair of huge double doors that looked even heavier owing to the heavy velvet lining the door. And next to them was the elevator that was definitely missing on the second floor.

The elevator announced an arrival with a ding. Inside

was an elderly gentleman standing tall with a benevolent look on his face. The glass door parted, and the man walked out toward Jin-kyung with a smile on his face. Generic white shirt, gray pants, shiny black shoes. He reached into his inside breast pocket casually as if looking for a pen or a cigarette case, pulled out a glittering pistol, and held it up to Jin-kyung's forehead.

"And you are?" he asked. Voice deep and rich in timbre, yet clear. Gray hair, wrinkles around the eyes, uncannily clear pupils. He had a face that did not reveal his age.

"Where's Do-kyung?" Jin-kyung asked instead of answering. "And what's happened to Woomi?"

The man cocked his head to one side. "Who?"

He wasn't pretending. He told her that he really didn't know who Do-kyung was. He didn't know Woomi, and he didn't know Jin-kyung. Jin-kyung was thrown by this response.

"If you people don't know, then who does?"

"*You people?*" The man laughed. "I haven't introduced myself, have I? I'm the Chief Secretary of the Office of Ministers. I maintain the office, prepare press releases for the Spokesperson, and take care of these irritating chores."

The Chief Secretary, holding eye contact with Jin-kyung, pulled his chin down toward his chest as if to say, *Your turn*. Jin-kyung was intimidated by his casual attitude, but didn't want to appear weak.

Jin-kyung pushed the barrel of his pistol with her forehead. "I didn't come all this way to see *you*! Where are the ministers?"

His pistol still against Jin-kyung's forehead, he undid the safety as casually as if fastening a button or pulling up a zipper.

"Did your husband die? Or your kid? Sick parents? Lose a job? And you think the ministers did it? There are lots of people like you, and that's called being delusional. And, again, who the hell are you?"

A draft came in through the open windows. The glass beads of the chandelier tinkled, sounds as clear and high as the comb and pins of a music box. Dry wind evaporating the sweat from her blouse, the smell of fresh grass, the smell of earth. Amazing peace. Something welled up inside her.

"Woomi is dying. The Saha Estates will be knocked down soon. And where the hell is Do-kyung?"

Shouting, Jin-kyung lunged toward the man and grabbed him by the collar. She was choking him, but he didn't pull the trigger. The four others rushed forward, the safeties on their guns clicking off loudly, but the man raised his left hand to keep them back.

His right hand still holding the pistol, which still was resting on Jin-kyung's forehead, he squeezed out the words, "Sounds like . . . there's something . . . you want to know. You'll have to . . . let go of me . . . to get an answer, no?"

A man capable of not firing a loaded weapon even when under threat. Getting out every last word even as the hands around his neck gradually cut off his air. Jin-kyung was beginning to be frightened of him. Her grip loosened, and the man shoved her away. Standing straight as before, he pulled at his tie and cleared his throat.

"Retreat," he said to the four still aiming at Jin-kyung. "I'll have a talk with her and send her back."

The four retreated down the steps, still aiming at Jin-kyung. The man raised his gun high above his head, struck Jin-kyung's forehead with the butt, and kicked her below the ribs with his heel. Jin-kyung doubled over and flew back.

He said, enunciating every word, "Dumb bitch. You trying to strangle me? You got a fucking death wish?"

He shoved his face in Jin-kyung's and asked, "It wasn't too difficult getting here, was it? This is not a hard place to find. Not a hard place to get into. I heard you hurt several people on the way for no good reason. You know this already, but your guide is dead."

The woman. The part of her that was bearing the harshest weight gave out with a crack, and Jin-kyung crumpled. Tears fell. In the mirage created by the tears, the woman was Woomi, then Do-kyung, then Jin-kyung herself.

Pistol still aimed at Jin-kyung's head, he stepped aside and gestured at the large door with his chin.

"Conference room."

The plum-colored velvet that covered the doors had turned pale with dust, but the long vertical door handles made of metal were polished to a shine. The shine had faded only in their centers, where the handles would have been grasped many times over. Jin-kyung clenched her fists but couldn't take a step. She'd come this far to open that door. And yet something inside her balked.

The man mocked Jin-kyung as she stood hesitant. "Yeah, I've heard of the Saha Estates. I heard what's happening.

Woomi? Do-kyung? Never heard of them. If you're curious, go have a look. Go on, pull the handle."

A sealed box containing all sources of human suffering. A woman who opens the box out of curiosity. Greed, hate, disease, death, and catastrophe all rush out. Pandora quickly closes the box, in which hope is the only thing that remains. An old cliché.

Jin-kyung took a deep breath and stepped forward. The wooden floor creaked under her foot. One step. And another, and another. Her heart raced with tension and fear. Eyes shut, she grabbed the long handles, one in each hand, cold against her palms. Jin-kyung pulled hard.

VISTA OF NOTHING.
No conference room.

THE DOORS WERE installed on the outer wall of the building. Outside the doors was an unobstructed view of the back of the property. Leaves of great trees undulated in the wind like waves and sunlight flickered as it filtered through. Jin-kyung couldn't believe that it was a straight drop under her feet, and almost took a step.

"Where are the ministers?"

"Not here."

"So where are they now?"

"There were no ministers to begin with."

Jin-kyung whirled around and seized him by the collar. "Liar! Where are the ministers?"

"Have you ever seen them? Either in real life or on TV or in photographs? Heard sound clips of them?"

Jin-kyung let go. Rolling his eyes, the man fixed his collar.

"I haven't had any visitors from the Saha Estates in a long time. I guess life is getting a little too easy for you people these days."

"Someone else came from Saha?"

"Last winter, I think. Guy with short hair, dark skin, about your age."

Jin-kyung couldn't imagine who that was. The Saha men around Jin-kyung's age were all short-haired and dark-skinned. Jin-kyung's face was flushed with confusion and frustration. He saw this and grinned.

"There was a researcher who stole all the data, specimens, and samples from the lab and came barging in here. I hear he's the custodian there now. The research center would like the material back."

The old man. *I see.* Jin-kyung thought of his old eyes, the strong grip as he grabbed her by the arm, and his nonchalant tone, which could be read as arrogant or wary. Her mouth went instantly dry as she remembered the taste of the Darjeeling tea he'd brewed for her.

"Give him my regards," said the Chief Secretary, sauntering over to the elevator.

"You want me to just go back to Saha?"

"You came to see the Council of Ministers, you found out there is no such thing. If you pull something so stupid again, the people you care about will pay. Return things to the way they were. Return to your place, do your part. Like they all did."

He pressed the elevator button and waved her over. Jin-kyung blankly followed. On the other side of the glass doors, she saw black wires slowly rising and pulling up a transparent elevator car that looked like an incubator. Jin-kyung's reflection on the glass doors burned white from the sunlight pouring in, so bright the outlines of her face were invisible. She saw Woomi's face in hers. Complexion so pale as to be blue, colorless lips, half-open eyes showing the whites.

If I step into that incubator, will I be reincarnated? As what?

The elevator doors opened, but Jin-kyung didn't get in. "They all went back quietly?" she asked the Chief Secretary.

He nodded. "Actually, there was one woman who attacked when she found out everything. That must have been over thirty years ago. She came here looking for her son, who went to work one morning and never came back, if you can believe it. She lunged at me with a small utility kitchen knife, which I blocked on instinct. She wound up stabbing herself in the face, right under her eye. I heard she ran away from the hospital. I'll bet she died. Well, she must be old enough to be dead of old age by now."

One face came to Jin-kyung's mind. And one question: "Whose decision was it to tear down the Saha Estates?"

"Who? Well, I can tell you there was no council meeting. Everything was decided before it came to that. The Spokesperson was just the messenger."

"Then who the hell are you?"

"Chief Secretary. I manage the Office of Ministers, prepare the Spokesperson's reports, and take care of tiresome things. Like you. I have no power. I'm just privy to a very big secret. A secret that everyone already knows on some level."

Her palm pressed against the wall, Jin-kyung said evenly, "She's not dead."

"What?"

"Not dead. That person who cut her own face thirty years ago. She's old, her hands shake, but she's alive. She uses an expensive fountain pen, a pretty cigarette case, and always wears a nice shade of lipstick. She hasn't forgotten you, either."

Jin-kyung thought of the old temp agent who led her to this place without asking a single question. Of the custodian who came back to Saha where Woomi was, of Granny Konnim who raised Woomi and Wooyon, of Sara who hid Do-kyung at her place. Of the public servant who burned the heptagram flags, the woman from decades ago who folded a paper boat and taped it up at the Parliament, and Ia's mother who said she did not sell her son. Jin-kyung thought of Su, who chose Do-kyung.

The Chief Secretary was distracted as he searched his memory. Jin-kyung attacked. She shoved his gun arm back and pounced, crashing to the floor with him. Four shots were fired in the tangle. One hit the glass, the second a vase, and the other two ricocheted off walls. He lost grip of the gun, which slid spinning across the floor.

Jin-kyung sank her teeth into the Chief Secretary's shoulder. His shirt was soaked with blood as she ripped a chunk of flesh off. The man lay on the floor in agony, and Jin-kyung picked up the gun.

"You're wrong," Jin-kyung said, pistol aimed at his head. "They did not go back to the way they were. And I will live out the rest of my days with Woomi and Do-kyung."

THE WIND BLEW. The large gingko tree guarding the Office of Ministers shook violently. The leaves, not yet yellow, fell to the ground. A butterfly flew over and alighted on a fallen leaf with its wings open. Vibrant yellow. Black whirls like a pair of eyes on the open wings. Feelers growing wide and tapering off at the tips looked like two feathers of a tiny bird adorning its head.